THERE'S NO SEA IN SALFORD

20

THERE'S NO SEA IN SALFORD

by Philippa Hawley

To Jane

best wishes

Philippa Hawley

Acknowledgements

Sincere thanks to Catherine and Jamie Dodds, Ginny Waters, Jane Olorenshaw and the wonderful friends who read endless drafts along the way – Natasha, Bill, Pippa, Mark, Faith and Tom, as well as Clinton, Victoria and Thomas.

ISBN 978-0-9570850-5-3

Published by Wivenbooks 2013
www.wivenhoebooks.com
Book and cover design by Catherine Dodds

In memory of Dorothy
1920–2004

Author's note

As a result of the Indian Ocean tsunami on 26 December 2004 approximately 33,320 people lost their lives in Sri Lanka. 21,411 people were injured and 516,150 people were displaced. Only Indonesia suffered more. The tidal wave affected the east coast of the country in particular.

Civil war in Sri Lanka between 1983 and 2009 caused over 80,000 deaths and suffering to many more. The twenty-five years of violence also damaged the economy and tourism. Nevertheless, Sri Lanka remains a captivating island of palm-tree lined beaches, and is abundant with spiritual, religious and historic remains.

That is all true – however this story is a work of fiction, as are the characters within it.

1

Kiri had to really concentrate to hear the music on the radio that morning – she was having one of her bad days. It was Boxing Day 2004 and she was home alone. The Christmas season was never easy for her – the days were short and the evenings long. For a non-Christian in a home without children it all seemed rather pointless. The endless children's films on TV highlighted her loneliness and the Christmas carols on the radio jarred her nerves. She turned up the volume on Radio 3. She'd struggled with her hearing for two years now, ever since Raja had struck her across the side of her head. She had bled from her ear that night, and never regained full hearing. At the time Raja wouldn't take her to the doctors – he told her he was too ashamed.

'My dear wife, I am so sorry, so very sorry. Please forgive me – please, please. It will not happen again. I am ashamed of the man I have become, the man you have turned me into,' he whined.

At the time Kiri thought how unfair that statement was. She hadn't turned him into anything. None of this was her fault. After the assault he had tried to be nicer to her for a while, but it didn't last – actually it was better when he ignored her. He still didn't allow her out of the house alone, he still kept the phone for incoming calls only, he still kept his study door locked, but at least he hadn't hit her for some time and was generally less demanding in the bedroom.

That Boxing Day morning Raja had gone off for a long day as on-call surgeon at the Salford Royal Hospital. He was getting fed up with the extra duty days that his colleagues put upon him, but he did enjoy the extra money. As a staff grade surgeon he was lower down the pecking order than he'd expected after all these years in England. He should have been a consultant by now with a juicy private practice, living in a big house with a housekeeper and a gardener – maybe even a driver to ferry him around. Those were his expectations – his dreams.

He'd proudly brought his pretty, young wife over in 1979, to live in married quarters at the Royal, and here he still was, twenty-five years later, stuck in a rut, failing to progress, and with a faded, useless wife. She was his housekeeper and there was no need for a gardener with only a tiny suburban back yard. It must be her fault – she's holding me back with her simple ways and her depression and poor health, he often thought.

'Bye, Kiri. I want my dinner on the table at seven,' were his departing words, as he left her alone in the chilly, drab house to face another day. Kiri tried to convince herself that she liked to be alone, when she could hear the music on the radio more clearly. Raja had scared away any friends she'd had, and she found it hard to go out on her own now, afraid of a panic attack in public. The radio was her friend, and music one of her few pleasures in life. The radio, her little flute and her sewing kept her going. She hummed a melancholy tune as she plodded round the house dusting and planning the menu for that evening.

A news flash suddenly interrupted Elgar's cello concerto. She stopped still in order to hear the voice of the news-reader, and instantly knew that something monumental was happening. Her heart lurched within her chest until she thought it would stop beating. Her breathing quickened to a high panting and she felt her limbs tremble. That was how she learnt the terrible news of the Boxing Day tsunami in the Indian Ocean and she felt the cloud over her grey house darken.

2

That same Boxing Day morning Penny and Clive said goodbye to Pen's sister and her husband, and thanked them for a wonderful Christmas. They'd eaten well, played charades and enjoyed the old-fashioned TV films. They went to church on Christmas morning and sang carols with gusto, full of the joys of the season.

They loaded their two teenage children, Hettie and Theo, into the back of the car with the box of presents, and set off to Northampton for the next stage of the Christmas celebrations and a visit to Clive's parents. Hettie and Theo were listening to their MP3 players and, realising that conversation would be limited, Penny switched on the car radio. She had to turn it up to hear the dramatic news that was unfolding. Clive stopped the car at the next lay-by and they listened with horror to the information coming in about the tragedy and destruction caused by an enormous tsunami crossing from Indonesia to Sri Lanka and Southern India. The children even took off their headphones to listen.

The four of them sat in silence, listening to the descriptions coming out of the radio, unable to visualise the wave that was sweeping across the Indian Ocean. They all knew how much Penny loved Sri Lanka. They teased her every time she mentioned that she'd spent three months there as a medical student on an elective study period in 1978. They pretended they were bored with stories about the trip, but secretly were rather interested and impressed. Now they listened without teasing. Clive decided to drive on, but kept the volume on the radio turned up high.

'We'll get to Northampton and put the telly on straightaway,' he said to Penny and patted her knee. 'Mum and Dad won't mind if we're a bit distracted. They know how you're obsessed by anything to do with Sri Lanka.'

Penny shivered and sat quietly listening to the growing scale of the disaster in disbelief. She'd always intended to go back to the island – the Pearl of the Indian Ocean – but had never managed it. Her life in England as a doctor, wife and mother had taken over. Now she desperately wanted to return, and that night in her in-laws' guest bed she started to talk to Clive about volunteering and returning with one of the aid organisations. Clive was not convinced this was a good idea – it might not be so easy to up sticks and go, but knowing his wife's desire to help others, he kept his thoughts to himself.

Penny couldn't get to sleep in the big comfortable bed, with Clive snoring next to her. She kept thinking of the weeks she'd spent in Sri Lanka with Jean, her fellow traveller, and wondered how all the people they had met there were coping. In particular she remembered the smiling face of Kiri, the young healthcare assistant who'd helped them enjoy their time in Kandy. She was sure Kiri's family came from Batticaloa, on that badly affected east coast.

By the time Penny and Clive got home after the Christmas break it was apparent that many lives had been lost since Boxing Day in those eastern parts. Homes were destroyed and schools and infrastructure swept away, in places already suffering since the insurrection in the 1970s and war of attrition since. New pictures of the recent destruction appeared daily in the papers and Penny and Clive responded by making a large donation to the Disasters Emergency Committee. They returned to their GP practice in the middle of a flu outbreak, and were so involved in looking after their own patients that thoughts of volunteering in Sri Lanka slowly faded, just as Clive thought they would.

Penny continued to think about Sri Lanka, and one evening she climbed up to the loft, where after much searching she found the dusty old box she was looking for. She brought it down to the kitchen.

'Look, Clive, I've found the box of all my old photos and a diary from 1978,' she announced. 'And here are the airmail letters I sent to my mum from Sri Lanka and her replies. She kept every one of them and returned them to me when I got back. Look, there's a faded picture of me with Jean – we look so young. Oh, and here we are with Kiri at the Elephant Orphanage – look how I tower over them both.'

'You always mention Kiri,' Clive remarked. 'She must have been quite special – pretty wasn't she? Whatever happened to her? Didn't you say she came to England after marrying that Indian surgeon?'

Penny spent the rest of the evening with Clive and a bottle of dry white wine, reminiscing about her three months in Sri Lanka, and this time Clive listened with interest and without his usual sarcastic albeit good-natured teasing. The next evening she read her diary and the creased blue airmail letters, and that's when her memories came back to life. Her mother's familiar writing pulled at her heart strings. She was horrified at how much she'd forgotten about the trip, and even more horrified that she'd lost touch with Kiri, and so rarely contacted Jean. Jean had been one of her best friends at university, but their careers and respective husbands had led them off in different directions, so communication was now reduced to a card and a letter each December.

Penny rifled through this year's Christmas cards in the recycling pile and found Jean's, with an up-to-date phone number inside. There's no time like the present, she thought, and she dialled the number.

'Dowling here,' barked Daniel Dowling, sounding rather fierce as he answered the phone, and Penny remembered why the two husbands hadn't always hit it off.

'Hi Daniel – it's Penny here, Penny Huxtable – Happy New Year to you. Is Jean there for a quick chat?'

'My goodness, Pen – long time no hear. Yes, Happy New Year to you. How's Clive? And the kids? Good. No, I'm afraid Jean's out at a breast care meeting. She'll be back about nine. I'll get her to call you. Great stuff,' he boomed and was gone.

Penny browsed through the bits and pieces she'd collected in Sri Lanka – brochures and tickets, postcards and photos. She still kept some little trinkets on an old printers' tray in her study, and had a batik-printed sarong squashed away somewhere in a drawer. It set her wondering about the life her old friend Jean was now living.

Jean was petite and dark-haired and very bright, with a quietly determined quality, which grew all the more focussed once she met Daniel. She'd met him during her senior house officer job in Guildford and they were married within a year. Daniel was a little older, and from a wealthy medical family. He was well on the way to a successful career in orthopaedics when they married, and they soon settled in Surrey. Penny met Clive about the same time and they'd moved around for a couple of years, before finding their GP practice in Essex. Only a hundred or so miles away, thought Penny – I must make more effort.

Penny recalled that Jean's famous determination saw her through her junior jobs and beyond, and she too became a successful surgeon – that much sought after creature, a female breast surgeon. It always amazed Penny that Jean managed to produce three lovely children along the way. Penny felt her life as a GP in practice with her husband was much more conducive to family life, and even she'd needed a series of nannies and au pairs to help bring up their two children. Still, Hettie and Theo had turned out pretty well, even if she said so herself.

The phone jolted her away from her musings, and Jean's voice rang out with just a hint of a Yorkshire twang breaking through the cultured southern accent she'd acquired after twenty years in Surrey with Daniel.

'Hi stranger, how are you?' piped Jean. 'Happy New Year. What are you up to?'

'Hi, Jean, I just really wanted to talk to you and to catch up. I've been thinking so much about Sri Lanka since the tsunami and I dug out my old diary from our trip,' replied Penny. 'It's made me think of all the people we met there, especially Kiri and her family in Batticaloa.'

'Yes – me too. Isn't it awful? I've been talking to Daniel about it since Boxing Day and wondering whether to phone you. Why don't we get together in London for lunch one day soon? We need a proper chat. I have a day off next Wednesday. Can you get away then?'

'Wednesday would be really good. It's my half day so should be no problem, and Clive will cover me for an early get-away. Let's meet at 1 o'clock at Carluccio's and bring your diary.'

3

Kiri sat for most of that Boxing Day watching the TV screen and hoping in vain that she might see pictures from Batticaloa. She felt too shocked by the whole event to cry, and too anxious to do anything useful. She'd have liked to phone Raja, but the house phone wouldn't allow out-going calls. Raja had stamped on her mobile phone last year in one of his rages and, having smashed it to smithereens, refused to allow her a replacement. She had no real friends, and couldn't go out alone. If she did manage to get out as far as his hospital across the city he would be furious that she'd disturbed him. She didn't know what to do, so she did nothing. That's not quite true – she prayed as she had never done before and berated herself for being so useless.

Kiri prayed and talked to whichever God would listen to her. She had been brought up a Buddhist, but at a time like this any God would do. Raja was an Indian Tamil, brought up as a Hindu, but he had no time for religion in the bitter world he now inhabited. Since they'd come to England neither Kiri nor Raja had enjoyed much of a spiritual life. Kiri tried to remember the Buddhist teachings she'd heard as a child, but they didn't seem to help her. The teachings were muddled in her mind, but she did remember thoughts of kharma, suffering and rebirth that seemed to fit somehow. Maybe this was her time of suffering and one day there would be a rebirth.

She knew a little of the Hindu faith through early lessons from Raja, but they didn't seem to help her at this time of crisis either. He'd talked about reincarnation, the sanctity of marriage and disapproval of divorce. He'd suggested that in his Hindu eyes he owned his wife. She knew there must be more to it, as this was one of the world's great religions, and she imagined the selfish Raja had only told her the things that were relevant to him. There was nothing there to comfort her. In the end she prayed to a generic God, a God of peace and healing and compassion, and she hoped that God was there listening to her, and watching over her mother in Batticaloa.

That long lonely day before Raja came home Kiri thought about her life, and how it hadn't turned out as she'd expected. She and Raja had been so excited to come to England in 1979. The civil war was making life difficult, especially in the north and east of the country, and a Tamil husband with a Sinhalese wife might well give rise to trouble. It was good to be removed from the conflict and get Raja to Europe to consolidate his career. The optimism they'd shared on arriving in England lasted just a few short years, before fading away.

Kiri had been a healthcare assistant at a missionary clinic in Kandy when they met. She had hoped to train as a nurse once she'd earned some money to supplement what her mother could provide. Her widowed mother worked as a school cook and didn't earn much, but was keen for her daughter to advance herself, so she allowed Kiri to leave home to go to Kandy when the chance of work arose. It was a way to make Kiri's dream of becoming a nurse come true, and the director of the mission assured her that her little girl would be kept safe there, well away from the troubles in the north and east.

The mission was situated alongside the lake in Kandy. Kiri had always lived by the sea and loved the water's energy. The lake was not quite the same but would do for now – it was pretty enough and brought freshness to the air. She shared a room with two junior nurses and they ate their meals in a little staff-room. The food was entirely vegetarian – no tea or coffee was allowed, and certainly no alcohol. Kiri missed her tea, but otherwise settled in well. She fondly remembered two visiting medical students from England, Penny and Jean, who came for a month, and stayed in the room next door to the nurses. They seemed to find the restricted diet more of a challenge and had coffee withdrawal headaches at first. Penny and Jean were only a couple of years older than Kiri but they seemed much more worldly-wise. Kiri enjoyed chatting with them and practising her already proficient English. Penny and Jean loved to ask Kiri questions about her country, and often invited her to accompany them on days out to help as a guide and interpreter. The three young women visited all the local sights – the Temple of the Tooth, the Botanical Gardens at Peradeniya, and the nearby Elephant Orphanage, where Penny took lots of happy photographs with her little Kodak camera – and they always treated each other to a cup of tea on their outings.

Kiri was bright in her work, but innocent and naive when it came to men, and Penny and Jean often teased her about a serious young Indian doctor who came to the clinic once a week from the General Hospital, to help out, and who seemed to fancy her. In Kandy her mother and two brothers had kept a close eye on her and she had not been allowed to meet young men from outside the family, so the growing attentions of the handsome, if rather short and dumpy, young doctor were flattering, even thrilling. One day he was assisting the surgical director, Mr Fernandez, with a tricky gall bladder operation, with the students observing and Kiri assisting the scrub nurse. The young surgeon's dark eyes flashed at Kiri over his mask and he thought he saw a blush rise up from the rounded cheeks behind her mask, which excited him.

After the demanding operation was over, they retired to the staff-room to refresh themselves with some cooling juice and Raja introduced himself to the pretty little healthcare assistant. On his weekly visits Raja started to seek out Kiri and always politely asked how she was getting on. One day he told her he was preparing for an important exam, his FRCS exam to become a surgeon, and Mr Fernandez was going to give him extra tutorials in the evenings, so he hoped he might see her more often. He told her she was cute as a button and she would make a great nurse one day. She remembered the butterflies in her stomach taking off when he said that, and he enjoyed seeing that exciting blush on her cheeks once more.

Penny and Jean had gone back to England by then and Kiri wished they were there to talk to – they would have helped her and told her how to react to his advances. She didn't want to seem too forward, but then again she didn't want to put him off.

He was about ten years older than her, she knew that much, and he was of course Indian, not Sinhalese, but she thought surely that didn't matter if they liked each other. He was so nice to her in private, full of flirtatious compliments, so she easily forgave the coolness he displayed in public, blaming it on professional courtesy. She remembered exchanging a few letters with Penny and Jean about him, but the time lag and the distance involved made any real discussion impossible. She felt alone with this new sensation and, flattered by his attentions, she convinced herself that they were in love.

Kiri was missing her mother in Batticaloa, as well as her English friends. She started to look forward to Raja's visits as the highlight of her week, and one day when they were alone in the staff-room she allowed him to kiss her and fondle her breasts through her uniform. How was Kiri to know that he had a fiancée in town – a fiancée from a well-to-do Indian family who were friends of his parents, and with whom he was due to have an elaborate wedding in Bangalore that summer? It had escaped his mind to inform the pretty little plaything of this important detail.

Raja and Kiri got too brave and started to walk out together in the evenings after work, and they became more intimate, despite a warning from Mrs Fernandez, the observant wife of the surgical director. Unbeknown to Kiri, Mrs Fernandez was not the only one to notice, and word got out to Raja's fiancée, Charmina. She immediately called off the wedding – the wedding Kiri knew nothing about.

Looking back Kiri realised that Raja went into damage limitation mode – too proud to show the hurt he felt. His Indian family had turned their backs on him, rejecting him for being so stupid as to offend Charmina's high-class family and ruin his chances of a good marriage. His brother, now a dentist and the favourite son, was too busy establishing his own career and was preparing to go to Canada to work. Raja determined that he would not lose his professional reputation as well as his family – he needed to get to England to advance his career.

Years later during a particularly nasty row, Raja had spilled out the whole sorry tale of their rudimentary courtship, as much to hurt Kiri as to explain himself. After the wedding he and Charmina were to move to England where he had secured a position as a surgical registrar in Salford – and they had been offered married accommodation at the hospital. If Charmina would not go with him, with her high and mighty ways, he decided he could take Kiri instead. He could be very persuasive and she would marry him at the drop of a hat – she could be moulded to his ways far better than the head-strong Charmina. He would lure Kiri away with the promise of enrolling her on a nurse training programme. She would give him the children he desired, pretty children, and so what if the nurse training never happened, she could always work as a healthcare assistant and look after his home? A Hindu man needed a good wife to look after him, serve him and look after his children. Kiri could be his housekeeper with benefits.

None of these calculations had mattered in the end, because Kiri got pregnant sooner than planned. Raja had to marry her in haste, and straight after the wedding they flew off to Manchester for their honeymoon. Kiri never told her mother she was pregnant, just that she was going to England to train as a proper nurse. Her new husband would look after her and they would send money home. Kiri made a fleeting visit to Batticaloa to say goodbye to her tearful mother who, still heartbroken at missing the wedding, was unable to change the girl's mind about leaving. Kiri's rose-tinted glasses were too powerful and the guilt she felt at leaving her mother was temporarily shielded by her misplaced love for Raja. Here she was nearly twenty-five years later locked in this place, so far from her homeland, estranged from her mother and the beautiful tropical seas of her memory. How could any God make that beautiful sea so cruel, she thought as the tears started to flow?

4

On Boxing Day evening Kiri found herself sitting in semi-darkness with no light apart from the flickering of the television screen and the orange, ghoulish glow from a street-light outside. She hadn't even drawn the curtains and the room looked tired – gloomy and grey, just like her. She felt exhausted with doing nothing. She hadn't even prepared the vegetables for dinner. She was cold with the inactivity of the day and drained by the emotion of it.

In between news bulletins Kiri allowed herself to think more about the losses she'd endured in her forty-four years on earth. Shortly after arriving in England in 1979 she'd lost her baby when she was eighteen weeks pregnant, and with that she lost her youth, her innocence and her hope. Raja seemed sympathetic towards her at first but then became distant. He told her it was hard enough fitting in with English ways at the hospital, and announced that it was for the best there was no baby to complicate their lives before they were fully settled. Kiri thought this callous – her grief was raw and persistent and all enveloping. It could not be rationalised, and there could be nothing 'best' about it. Raja's patience ran out when she didn't perk up, and he told her to pull herself together and get over it. When she got pains deep in her pelvis, he made light of them and ignored her request to call the midwife or the health visitor. Only when she became seriously ill, with soaring fevers, did he take her back to hospital. She had a deep-seated infection and had to have intravenous antibiotics and an operation. He seemed embarrassed, even ashamed, and told her it made him feel dirty.

Raja buried himself unhappily in his work and Kiri kept house as best she could in her enfeebled condition. Whenever she talked about applying for nurse training Raja told her she was still too weak. He no longer took her out – he just wanted her at home, cooking and cleaning for him, and demanded his marital rights in the bedroom, even if she was in pain. She stoically tolerated this in the hope they might grow close again, as they had once been in Sri Lanka, and more than anything hoping for another baby but no baby came.

After five years of trying it was heartbreakingly apparent that Kiri had not only lost her longed-for baby but also her fertility. Again Raja wouldn't take her to the doctors for help, considering such things private between couples. To her it seemed the gods didn't want them to have children and they were being punished for the lies they had told when they left for England. By then she'd been told about Raja's previous engagement and he taunted her saying she had trapped him into marriage. The day she answered back that it was quite the opposite was the day he beat her for the first time. She learned not to answer back and gradually she became little more than his housekeeper and slave. He wouldn't allow her to work outside the house and she felt worthless, unable to be a proper wife or a mother and unable to help in the outside world. She'd lost her hope of becoming a nurse, and her self-esteem withered away, as did her prettiness and her open smile.

Despite the long hours Raja worked at the hospital he found it hard to progress. He was a good technical surgeon, but he lacked bed-side manner and found it difficult to make friends with his colleagues. Over the years Kiri saw him travel up and down the country attending interviews for consultant posts, but he never got beyond the short-lists. He had few friends but still seemed to avoid coming home to her.

Kiri knew Raja received a good salary and she often wondered where it all went – she certainly didn't see much of it.

He gave her a small housekeeping allowance and asked to see receipts for everything she purchased. He discouraged wasting money on bus fares, so she didn't go far from home. Then one day he decided she shouldn't go out alone, and from then on he did the weekly shop with her. She lost even that little piece of freedom.

It had occurred to her that he might be paying for sex elsewhere and she suspected that he might gamble – where else could the money be going? After five years in a hospital-owned rented house they did buy their own house, and for a while this cheered them both up. They bought a three-bedroomed semi in a nice quiet street and it had a small back garden – more of a yard with a strip of earth around it, where Kiri grew herbs and a few vegetables among the flowers. They furnished the house comfortably but with little style, and they never had visitors. Kiri enjoyed needle-work and embroidery during her long days at home, and some of her pieces adorned the walls. She still played sad, soulful songs on the little flute she'd brought from Sri Lanka, but never if Raja was around – she had no need to give him reason to criticise. When he was there she stuck to watching TV or reading the books Raja chose for her – straightforward books, carefully vetted to keep her occupied but not to give her bright ideas. He didn't want her to get above her station, so he kept his more racy books locked away in his private study. He steered her away from any literature with feminist tendencies, but decided good old-fashioned detective stories and crime fiction were acceptable. These were the shows she enjoyed on TV too, as well as chat shows – Raja couldn't control what she learned about human behaviour from these.

Raja's study was his personal space, and the locked door meant she couldn't even go inside to clean. He spent hours in there fiddling on his expensive computer. He'd also treated himself to a Rolex and an old Mercedes with a throaty-sounding engine. Perhaps these things, his boys' toys, were using up his money and not prostitutes or gambling after all, she liked to think.

* * *

Kiri heard the characteristic engine noise as it drew up that Boxing Day evening. Despite her less than perfect hearing she was tuned into this familiar sound. She sat up with a start, and hyperventilated when she realised his dinner was not made. The last time she'd neglected his dinner was the night he had ruptured her ear-drum. Now she held her breath as his key turned in the lock. She usually needed just a second to gauge his mood – it was alright tonight. In fact she thought he looked pretty calm – not surprising, as he had just extricated himself from a certain young lady's flat, after a deliciously warm encounter there. He hadn't caught the news – he'd been in theatre all day operating, so was unprepared for the urgent greeting;

'Raja, Raja. Thank goodness you are home. It's awful – dreadful! Look at the news. Look at the pictures. Whatever will we do?' Kiri shrieked at him and grasped his arm.

Raja took off his coat, poured himself a brandy and sat Kiri down on the settee next to him. He calmly absorbed the news and watched the terrible television pictures, noting the increasing death toll in Sri Lanka and Southern India in particular. His family, with whom he'd had very little contact since the unfortunate business with Charmina, still lived in Bangalore and should be safe. Kiri's mother in Batticaloa was much more at risk. Kiri's brothers now both lived and worked as taxi drivers in America, so Kiri's mama would be alone there.

'Raja,' begged Kiri. 'I must contact Mama. I must know if she is safe. I need to go home. Let me go home?'

'My dear woman, you cannot go home. You have no passport. It expired years ago,' replied Raja. 'Your nerves are so bad you couldn't cope with the journey, and we really can't afford the flight. There will be chaos in your country. They will not want any more mouths to feed and you're not strong enough to be of any practical help, so just be sensible and we'll make enquiries about your mama tomorrow. We'll get news somehow but let's sleep on it tonight. Look they've even put a number on screen for worried relatives to phone. I'll jot it down and call from my mobile in the morning once it's charged up.'

He sounded so reasonable that she had to accept what he said. He didn't even complain about the makeshift meal of rice and vegetables and she felt too tired to be suspicious of his mood. That night as she lay in bed next to her husband, Kiri became even more determined to get back home, whatever obstacles he put in her way. He'd prevented her going back even for a visit for the last twenty-five years – frightened that she would never return to England and he would lose face – or just because he could. Now things were different and she had to go – she just had to, and somehow she would find a way. The cloud that was hovering over her home seems to lift a little but it still didn't disperse.

5

The next morning Raja's mellow mood had passed. He overslept, and felt groggy after too much brandy. He'd forgotten to charge his mobile and of course the house phone took only incoming calls. He promised he'd phone the emergency enquiry number from work and call Kiri with any information. Then he left her alone, locked in the house, with no money in her purse, no means of escape and nowhere to go. The familiar feeling of helplessness washed over her once more, as she switched on the TV news. She wondered if he would remember to call. It would be a long day – he was usually late home if his day started with a bad mood.

Raja did indeed delay going home that night by calling in on Ria after his shift, not wishing to face his needy wife. He phoned Ria ahead of his visit to make sure she was home from work, and knowing she liked some notice of his arrival – it was best to stick to the rules with the lovely Ria.

She was Portuguese and worked part-time as a nurse on the Obs and Gynae unit. He'd met her at a hospital function about eight years before and they seemed to like each other's detached attitude to life. She'd lost her husband, Enrico, two years previously, and came to England for a new start. Raja and Ria both seemed like outsiders in the hospital, and drawn together by this, they became friends, then lovers in a situation that suited them both well. Ria was a little younger than Kiri, and pretty enough, with a open smile, and a need for regular sex. She knew Raja was unhappily married, but asked few questions and that suited him. She was good at acting the role of poor, lonely widow, and allowed Raja to make a financial contribution towards her rent, in return for staying overnight when on-call. Her flat was just opposite the hospital and safely within bleeping range. He enjoyed the warm atmosphere there more than that of his own home, but was careful not to overstay his welcome. Ria made it very clear that despite enjoying the benefits of their relationship, she liked her independence and valued having time to herself.

When he eventually did go home to Kiri that night, his dinner was dried out, having been kept warm in the oven for far too long. He lied that the emergency number was busy all day, and said he would try again later. He couldn't be bothered to talk to Kiri and went straight to his study after eating, leaving her with the washing up, as usual.

The anxious days lurched by and it was almost two weeks later when Kiri found out that her mother was alive. Her nattering had finally resulted in Raja making the call, to shut her up if nothing else. He discovered that Kiri's mother, Lali, had lost her home and her possessions but had kept her life. She was living in a temporary camp for homeless women and Raja promised to send money. Kiri doubted he would get round to it when he said that. She repeatedly begged him to help her go home to see her mother, but he continued to block her and became angrier each time she asked. Fear of his anger and of another beating held her back, but she made up her mind to add more to the savings she'd collected – kept back from the housekeeping allowance over the years. She kept her money stashed away at the back of the larder and called it her rainy-day pot – but of course every day seemed a rainy day in Salford. Oh how she missed the sparkling seas and sun of Sri Lanka she knew of old. She prayed the tsunami's damage could be overcome and her beautiful country restored.

* * *

Meanwhile in Sri Lanka Lali was doing alright. She'd been up country visiting her cousin when the wave came, so escaped the immediate danger but returned to find she had no home. Her small house near the beach had disappeared so completely that you couldn't even see where the foundations had been. Later Kiri heard that all she had left was an overnight bag and the clothes she stood up in. She was housed in a camp for homeless people at first, crammed in with hundreds of others. Lali was thankful to be alive amidst such chaos, and after a few days of confusion and uncertainty she decided to walk all the way back to the school where she had worked as a cook for many years. She knew there would be damage there and hoped she could be of some help. There was no use mouldering away in a camp when she could be helpful, she thought, and anyway she worried about getting ill in that place where hygiene was dreadful and food in short supply.

The school was built on a slope with some buildings on higher ground, and others at sea-level. Those lower buildings were flattened, and the school gardens flooded, but the headmistress's house, the office, one classroom and a hall-like dormitory block had defiantly stood their ground. Lali had been welcomed back with open arms and was invited to stay in the staff part of the dormitory. They'd soon put her to work in the kitchen, grateful that this elderly lady was back safe, and part of their loyal team once more. Food was limited here too, but Lali was resourceful and creative with whatever produce they could find. Here Kiri's mother was a valued survivor.

6

In mid January, just a couple of weeks after the tsunami, Penny and Jean met in Covent Garden and made their way to Carluccio's where they'd booked a table for lunch. They caught up with each other's family news – yes, the husbands were both well and working too hard, the children were all well and not working hard enough, but all had high hopes for bright futures. The women compared notes on work and the NHS, and on the whole all was well in middle-England in their middle-class worlds. They talked about how different it must be now in Sri Lanka since the tsunami and how unimaginable the wave must have been. They discussed stories they'd read in the papers written by British tourists who'd survived or lost family and friends in the disaster and they both shared an urge to go back there, or help, or do something.

They each ordered a glass of Pinot Grigio, then bruschette, followed by griddled tuna and salads. They were in no rush, so after the meal Penny brought out her 1978 diary and they settled down to a session of nostalgia. They flicked through the dog-eared pages and dragged events and scenes back to their memories. The waiters watched with resigned expressions, and topped up the ladies' coffee cups, realising they were in for a long afternoon.

Sadly Jean had lost her diary but Penny's gave them plenty to talk about and they felt close again after all those years. They recalled what a great time they'd had in that beautiful country, remembering the warmth and friendliness of the people they'd met. They often came across Kiri's name in the pages, and remembered the young nursing assistant who had befriended them in Kandy, and recalled her infectious smile.

Penny and Jean laughed when they talked about being dropped off at Victoria Station by their boyfriends at the time – Bob and Dave, and how they'd caught the coach to Heathrow with luggage for the next three months. They spent a moment wondering what had happened to Bob and Dave, and Jean commented that she'd have trouble packing for three months these days – their needs had been much simpler back then. They recalled feeling excited and terrified at the same time as they travelled eastwards, arriving at Colombo Airport after hours and hours in the air. An unforgettable hazy heat and a rich spicy smell had hit them when they stepped out on to the tarmac and into another world.

They remembered the lodgings they'd arranged with a Mrs de Rana in Park Road, through a contact at the medical school, and how nervously they'd looked around for Mrs de Rana's driver who was to meet them at Arrivals – how he'd driven them into the city past shacks along the roadside which sold cans of drink and coconuts and little else, and how ragamuffin children played on the scrub land in the shelter of palm trees. The girls had stayed with Mrs de Rana and her daughter Chrisanthi for four weeks, and had a work attachment on the children's ward at the nearby university hospital. Thank goodness the comfortable de Rana household was an English-speaking home, and Mrs de Rana had treated them like daughters. They'd shared a beautiful room with tall ceilings, and a fine brass fan wafted air over them as they slept. They ate with the family – spicy food that burned their throats and had to be tempered with cooling yoghurts until they got used to it. They never quite got used to curry sauce on the breakfast string-hoppers and had always asked for mango jelly instead.

At work things had been less comfortable – they saw things they'd never seen in England – tetanus, malaria, life-threatening gastroenteritis, extreme pneumonias and more. Children died when they should have lived and the doctors and nurses had to harden their hearts to the grieving mothers who never left, and slept beneath their children's beds. Penny and Jean found it hard to witness the suffering they saw.

They remembered being scared of the Professor of Paediatrics and worried she would find out when they played hooky and took off unannounced for a long weekend on a tourist trip to Trincomalee – in need of some light relief and recreation. In Trincomalee they'd stayed in lovely wooden huts on the beach, they swam in the ocean and ate wonderful baked crabs and drank beer – it had felt exciting and exotic, unreal – like a romantic film set. It was a shame Bob and Dave weren't there, they'd thought at the time – but at least the Professor never did find them out.

After a month in Colombo the girls had packed up and taken the train to Anuradhapura, for their second attachment. Here they'd stayed with a Sri Lankan physician, Ronni and his Australian wife, Bernie – short for Bernadette apparently. Bernie was a paediatrician and was expecting their first baby. She'd seemed to enjoy the company of the western girls with their cheerful chatter. Life had been relaxed in Ronni and Bernie's house, with unobtrusive servants looking after them. The food was good but simple, as was the decor, and they'd slept at night under draped mosquito nets. Plump mangoes and juicy pawpaws were growing outside in the front garden, and the girls used to pick their own breakfast from the trees. When they got back to England medical finals would be just three months away so Ronni had given them revision tutorials in the evenings while Bernie rested.

'I'm sure that's what got me through my final exams,' said Penny.

The girls' third and final attachment was in Kandy where they'd stayed at a mission hospital next to the lake, run by a Seventh Day Adventist surgeon and his wife. Here they revised surgery. The most striking thing they remembered about this clinic by the lake was that it was very smart – not at all what they imagined as a 'mission'. It had been more like a private hospital and they'd met visiting surgeons there from Kandy General Hospital. One day they'd gone to visit the outpatients department at Kandy General and couldn't believe the difference they found. At this hospital some of the patients walked miles to attend an appointment and waited in overcrowded waiting halls in overpowering heat. Some presented with enormous tumours that must have been growing for ages before they sought help, so making the surgeons' job that much harder. Penny and Jean saw pathology in the raw here and had learned far more than a text book could teach them. They'd returned to the comfortable mission clinic feeling guilty at the comfort there and more than a little shocked by what they'd seen at the hospital.

Now over more coffee, some twenty-six years later, Penny and Jean's thoughts turned to Kiri, and Penny produced a photograph of the three of them. Kiri in a pink sari, with her long hair tied back, looked pretty and petite with a smiling round face. Jean was just a little taller, with dark hair in a short bob, and burnished sun-tanned skin and Penny was taller still – freckle-faced with wavy light brown hair tied back with a scarf. The English girls both wore sundresses and sensible sandals and they all three looked happy. In the background an elephant and its keeper were bathing in the river – this was the image of their day out at the Elephant Orphanage. They remembered lots of other days out with Kiri – she was quite the travel agent. Penny and Jean had tried to repay her, buying her cups of tea (she seemed addicted to tea they recalled) and inviting her to go swimming with them to the pool at the Hotel Suisse next door to the clinic. Kiri always said she preferred to swim in the sea and had told them stories about the beautiful ocean at Batticaloa where she'd grown up, with tales about the fishermen there.

'I loved the elephants didn't you, but where, pray tell, did your freckles go to?' asked Jean, looking again at the fading picture.

'Ha ha, a combination of age and fine make-up has defeated them,' replied Penny, 'but how about Kiri – I do wonder how she is? When did you last hear from her? The last time I heard from her was about twenty years ago. I sent her my usual Christmas card, and tucked a little picture of Hettie as a new-born into it, but it was sent back marked 'Not known at this address'. I always wondered what happened – I guess she must have moved and never sent her new address. Shame really!'

'Oh, I think you did better than me at keeping in touch. We only exchanged a few letters in the early days after we got home. I did get a card saying she was in England having married that sleazy Indian chap, Raja, about a year later, but then nothing since. I feel bad about it really – she was so sweet and so kind to us in Sri Lanka, and we never returned the compliment in England.'

Penny sighed, 'I know, me too. In England we are so bad at returning hospitality to foreign visitors. Anyway what do you mean, that sleazy chap, Raja? He wasn't that bad was he?'

Jean groaned slightly, 'I thought he was pretty dreadful. He had no social graces whatsoever, in fact I'd say he was rude. I wondered what Kiri saw in him, although I suppose he was quite nice looking for a small man.'

'Jean, you can't say that!'

'Yes I can, it's true. Nice face, but that's about all. He did get his FRCS when he came to Salford you know, but I don't think he ever made consultant. I made some enquiries a year or two ago at a breast surgeons' meeting in London, when some of the Manchester team came down. They seemed to think he was a staff grade in Salford at the time, and had been for years. Actually one of my colleagues, Harry Rees from Carshalton, has just moved to the Christie Unit in South Manchester – they head-hunted him when their senior chap retired last year.'

'Good for Harry, but it sounds sad that Raja's got stuck in a bit of a rut. He and Kiri had such high hopes for life in England, but then again I did think they'd made a rushed decision about marrying and moving away so quickly. I got the feeling he was running away from something and poor little Kiri got caught up in it. Did you know she was pregnant and lost her baby?' Penny continued, 'I think we should try to find her again and see how she is. Whatever life has been like for her she'll be feeling pretty awful about the tsunami, and she'll be worried for her friends and family.'

'Yes, I knew she'd lost her baby. I gather she was quite ill afterwards. I agree – we should make an effort and get back in contact. It's so easy to get bogged down in one's own world – what with work and homes and families, but it's important to make space for old friends too,' said Jean.

'I think we need to do more than just get in touch with Kiri – we need to get back in touch with Sri Lanka. We must be able to do something useful, even if it's simply fundraising or raising awareness of the problems the country now faces – first the civil war and now the tsunami, it's all too much,' said Penny.

Jean agreed that now their careers and families were established they had more time for friends and fund-raising, and as each other's oldest friends they arranged another lunch meeting the following month in London. In the meantime they'd both put out feelers to try to find Kiri, and research any projects they could support in Sri Lanka.

7

A few days later Penny got an email from Jean, thanking her for lunch, and passing on some early results from her enquiries. She had already phoned her surgical colleague, Harry, in Manchester – he'd heard of a Mr Coomara who worked in Salford as a staff grade on the Gastrointestinal Unit, but had never actually met him. He told Jean he'd make further enquiries, but he had heard that Coomara was a rather odd chap – Indian, and kept himself to himself. It sounded like Raja, and Penny was excited to think he was still there and so easy to find. She suggested to Jean that they phone the hospital in Salford straightaway, but Jean was more circumspect, thinking they should wait for more information, so as not to put their size nines in it. Just because Raja was there it didn't mean Kiri was. They could be separated or divorced – anything could have happened. Clive agreed with Jean and urged patience – not his wife's best quality. Harry hadn't known anything about this man. He didn't know if he was married or had children, just that there was something odd about him. Perhaps he and Kiri had been divorced and that was why she'd gone off the radar.

At first Penny agreed, but after a few days her impatience got the better of her. The television and papers were still filled with the traumas of the tsunami and a rising death toll, so Sri Lanka was never far from her mind. She disappointed herself by not acting on her inclination to help, even though she checked the volunteer sites regularly. Instead she focussed her attention on the idea of finding Kiri. One afternoon when she had a half day off work, and the house was quiet, she picked up the phone and dialled the number for the Royal, in Salford. She introduced herself as Dr Huxtable and asked the telephonist for Mr Coomara. He was in theatre so Penny was put through to the GI department secretary, who took her number and said she'd ask Mr Coomara to call her back.

Two days later no return call had come, so Penny tried the secretary again. As luck would have it Mr Coomara was in the office next door, and she would try to put her through.

'Hello, Mr Coomara, Raja, is that you?' Penny asked cautiously. 'You may not remember me, but I think we met in Kandy in 1978. I was a friend of Kiri's. My name is Penny, Penny Huxtable, and with my friend Jean, I was on my elective at the Seventh Day Adventist Hospital by the lake.'

Raja took some time to reply, 'Mmm, I do vaguely remember you both. What do you want?' he said abruptly.

Penny wondered if Jean's opinion of his rudeness might be accurate after all, but she pressed on. 'We wondered how Kiri was getting on? We wanted to catch up with her. We were so concerned to hear of the tsunami, and we wanted to talk to her. Could you give me a number please so I can call her?'

'No, I don't think I can do that. She's a very private person and she's not been well. She might not want to speak to you. I'll tell her you called, goodbye,' and with that he hung up.

Something didn't feel right to Penny. If Kiri had been ill then surely a call from an old friend might be just what she needed. She wondered why Raja had been so short with her – perhaps he was just busy with work. She did hope she hadn't messed things up by phoning out of the blue. Damn, she realised she'd not given him her contact details. She phoned the secretary back and left her number for Raja to pass on to Kiri – that was the best she could do for now. That evening when she told Clive about her strange conversation with the reticent Mr Coomara, Clive teased her about her impatience and asked what she'd expected – an invitation to come and stay? The trouble was that no return call ever came from Kiri, just a short message from Raja asking her to leave them alone. What was that man trying to hide?

8

True to form, that night after Penny's call Raja arrived home in one of his foul moods. Kiri had no idea as to the cause of his mood but recognised it all too well and did her best not to upset him further. The last thing she wanted this week was a beating. She couldn't cope with that tonight, because tomorrow she had an appointment at the breast clinic. He was always quite careful not to mark her body or leave bruises that might show, he was always sorry afterwards, would comfort her, bathe her wounds, apply arnica to her bruises and swear it would never happen again, but she recognised the signs tonight and knew she was at risk. Thank goodness she'd made him a good dinner. He usually liked her chicken curry with okra and tomatoes, but tonight he criticised it, saying the chicken was tough and the flavours bland.

'Can't you do anything right?' he barked at her when she spilt a splash of sauce on the clean table cloth. 'You are a useless wife.'

His anger built and his words became cruel, making her blink back tears as he embarked upon one of his tirades. She knew she must not cry – that would inflame him more. She wondered where his anger came from – it seemed to rise up from a bottomless pit, never far from the surface. Then Raja's red mist truly exploded,

'All you have to do is keep house. All you have to do is look after me. You are not even burdened by children to run after – you who couldn't give me children, you who are so ugly with one breast that I have to turn your back to me when we have sex. What sort of a wife are you? I should have married the beautiful Charmina, and not played around with the likes of you. You are just an ignorant Sinhalese woman, with your sewing and your flute as your only friends.As a proud Tamil, I should never have married the likes of you. You have held me back in my career. I should have kept my beautiful Charmina – she would have made a perfect wife, and given me beautiful children. She would have looked so fine on my arm and enhanced my career. If you hadn't soiled me with your promiscuous body in Kandy, my life would have been good, not like this cold miserable existence we have in this suburb of Salford, in this depressing house.'

He raised his arm. In uncontrolled fury he swung at her. Kiri ducked down and dodged to one side. Instead of connecting with her head, Raja struck a glass vase on the shelf behind her. When Kiri dared to look up, she saw blood pouring from his wrist and he was panting hard. The sight of the blood stopped him in his tracks and he sank to his knees. In her calmest possible voice Kiri tried to sooth him,

'It's alright, husband – be still. I can fetch water and towels and clean this up. Stay quite still and cover your wrist with this clean hanky till I return.'

Kiri went to the kitchen to get water and antiseptic, and breathed a sigh of relief, having escaped a beating for tonight. The rage was over for today and she could attend her annual check-up at the clinic tomorrow without shame. She returned to the dining room and carefully cleaned the jagged cut.The main blood flow abated, but no matter how hard she pressed a slow, red ooze continued to creep through the hanky. Raja took over applying pressure, while Kiri tidied up the broken glass. At least there were no flowers and no water in the vase, she thought to herself – he had never ever bought her flowers, not even on their wedding day.

'I think you might need stitches, husband dear,' she said gingerly.

'Since when did I value your surgical opinion? No, I just need steri-strips. There are some in my study. Here, take the keys and bring me some from the top drawer of my desk, then lock the door after you,' he ordered.

Kiri went into his study for the first time in many years. She glanced around quickly – a little musty but surprisingly neat and tidy, she thought, considering she wasn't allowed in to clean. She found the dressings in the top drawer of his desk, and next to them spotted a spare key to the study door. She slipped this into her apron pocket, and returned to tend to her husband. Once he was patched up, she poured him a large brandy, suggesting it would help him sleep. Raja went to bed early, and Kiri finished tidying the kitchen with her mind working overtime. She patted her pocket to check the key was still there and its presence made her smile.

9

The following morning Raja got ready for work as usual, insisting he'd be fine. He ordered a taxi for Kiri and put her into it, giving her just enough money to pay for the return fare to the Christie Hospital in Manchester, with a little extra for a lunchtime snack. They were used to this routine and had replayed it often since she got breast cancer three years earlier. Raja always used the same taxi company, run by a trusted Indian family. Kiri sat like a little mouse in the back seat of the cab and the driver never spoke to her. She guessed those were Raja's orders.

Raja had seemed to have her best interests at heart when he suggested she'd be better looked after at the larger Manchester unit rather than at his own hospital in Salford, but she'd come to realise that he simply wanted to keep her far away from his territory. He wanted her to have no part in his working life in Salford – he wanted to hide her and keep her secret. He was ashamed of her.

Raja was heavily involved with Ria by the time the breast cancer came, and he wanted to keep the two women as far apart as possible. At first he'd given Ria the idea that he and Kiri were separated, and Ria seemed to accept this. She didn't question him and was simply happy to take his rent contribution, in exchange for those nights on call when he stayed with her. Ria didn't really need the money, but he seemed happy to pay for his comforts. She was pleased to have the flat to herself most of the time and certainly didn't want him moving in with her. She'd decided not to ask too many questions – it was so much simpler to leave things as they were.

In the early stages of Kiri's treatment Raja used to go with his wife to clinic, keeping up the pretence of the caring husband. She did think it odd when he booked her in under her maiden name of Kiribaba de Souza and then put his full name, Mr Raja Coomaraswamy down as her next of kin. He told Kiri that this was the custom in big hospitals in England, but she could tell the staff she was known as Kiri. Why he kept quiet about his own surgical career she never knew, and she didn't dare question him when it seemed he was being sympathetic towards her.

At the time of her diagnosis Kiri was listed for a mastectomy and axillary clearance, followed by radiotherapy. She still had the little tattooed spot on her chest where the radiation was focussed.She went through the treatment in a daze, but afterwards absolutely refused to have the chemotherapy they recommended. She was too full of fear – fear about how she'd cope with the side-effects, fear at how she'd cope with Raja if she felt ill with it. So even though her team of doctors and nurses tried to persuade her and told her she was putting her life at risk, she stuck to her guns, resolutely saying no. She convinced herself the radiotherapy was enough to kill off any bad cells remaining, and home she went with her blinkers on. She and Raja never discussed the subject again.

Her check-up appointments had gone well since that difficult time three years ago, so that morning with the taxi driver silent as stone in front of her, she travelled to the clinic with only a minor level of anxiety. She was never comfortable being out of the house alone, but was holding it together pretty well. Her left armpit felt sore when she put on her seatbelt, but she thought it was just from the lurching twist she'd made when avoiding Raja's fist the night before. She paid the driver and walked towards the clinic, her footsteps echoing down the tall corridors. The smell of polish and disinfectant made her feel light-headed and slightly queasy. People passed by with worried looks on their faces, avoiding the gaze of others in case they caught a look of distress or pain – or something more contagious perhaps. One rarely sees a happy smiling face in these places, thought Kiri – most people here are worried. She wondered how the doctors and nurses remained cheerful and positive – even if it was only on the surface she did appreciate their efforts.

At the clinic she was booked in to see one of the regular doctors, Dr Anne Ross, who had seen her on and off for three years. Dr Anne always seemed kind and concerned without being too pushy or nosy and Kiri liked her. Dr Anne spoke clearly so Kiri could hear her words and after a preliminary chat she politely asked if she could examine her. The doctor went quiet as she felt over and over again at a thickened, tender place in Kiri's left armpit.

'Have you noticed this tender spot before?' she asked.

'No – nothing different,' replied Kiri, suddenly wanting the examination to be over, and to run away.

'Is anyone here with you this morning, your husband perhaps?' Dr Anne went on, 'because I think we might need to check this little area out. It might just be scar tissue, but we can't be too careful.'

'No, today I am alone,' whispered Kiri. 'What do you need to do?'

'Well, first I'd like you to meet our new consultant, Mr Rees. Let's see what he thinks.'

'Oh, a man you say – I don't think so. Is this all really necessary? Let's leave it till next time. Let's see how things go. It might just settle down on its own.'

'Now Kiri, you know we can't just leave it. Come now – Mr Rees is an excellent doctor and a fine surgeon. He's moved to us from London and we're very lucky to have him. He's a gentleman – kind and thoughtful too. Will you see him?'

Kiri agreed and Dr Anne went off to fetch Mr Rees, leaving Kiri with a new clinic nurse she'd not seen before. The two women sat quietly, and exchanged shy and embarrassed smiles. The nurse passed Kiri a plastic cup of chilled water, and the glugging of the water dispenser broke the tense silence. Mr Ross breezed in like a charming whirlwind – tall and good-looking, with a golden tan and an open smile.

'Miss de Souza, or is it Mrs? Sorry,' he said, glancing at the notes. 'How nice to meet you – I'm Mr Harry Rees, your new consultant. Dr Anne would like me to look at this troublesome area under your arm. May I?'

The appointment stretched out, with Kiri being passed from one team member to the next. She met advisors, counsellors, nurses, clerks and doctors over the next couple of hours, and her calm young nurse, Ramona, shadowed her at every step like a kindly guard. It was arranged that Kiri would go back the following week, after a scan, for a biopsy and Nurse Ramona, her new friend, promised to be there with her. Ramona had spotted the vulnerability in this shy, reticent patient and felt sure she needed help. This woman needed more support, and where the heck was her husband anyway, thought Ramona.

In the team meeting at the end of the long busy clinic, Ramona expressed her concern to Dr Anne and the counsellor, and both promised to keep an eye on the little Sri Lankan woman the following week. Kiri left the clinic and skipped lunch. She didn't feel like eating – actually she still felt sick, so she saved her lunch money for the rainy-day pot, adding a little extra when the taxi driver undercharged her for the journey home.

That evening when Raja got home he asked how her appointment had gone, but his nose was already in the newspaper when she answered, and he didn't listen to the reply.

'Fine, thank you. I don't have to go back until the summer. A six-month follow-up appointment has been made,' she lied, horrified at the ease with which she could tell fibs these days. She'd turned down chemotherapy in the past, and she certainly didn't want it now – it might delay her getting back home to her mother and that was her main aim. She wouldn't care then if she died. As long as she was at home in Sri Lanka and had seen her mother once more, she would be content – no, she would be relieved – to die. She just had to work out how to escape from the prison Raja had created around her. She knew she would need help but at that moment she couldn't think of anyone she knew well enough to trust. She thought there was no such person. At least she did have the spare key to the study and she had a little money in her escape fund – not enough of course, but something of her own and that was a start. She racked her brain trying to think of a plan and realised the breast clinic provided her only means of contact outside the house.

10

Raja went off to work the next day, saying he'd stay at the hospital that night, as there was a clinical meeting at the postgraduate medical centre and it would finish late. Kiri was pleased – it meant she had plenty of time to explore his study and to think about her future.

She carefully opened the door, and checking every detail she slipped into the unfamiliar room, breathing in the weird musty smell again – a mixture of Raja's aftershave and old books. She was careful not to move or dislodge anything. She knew she must leave no evidence of the intrusion. She was amazed at the different world contained within this strange room. Here was a modern computer with a printer, and next to it on the desk a telephone with a dialling tone. Surely that meant she might be able to dial out, if only she knew who to call. She'd never used a computer but knew they had passwords, so the shiny white machine with its key-board wouldn't be much use to her.

She carried on exploring the desk top and looked at the jottings on Raja's notepad as well as in his desk diary – the name 'Ria' cropped up a lot. She opened his desk drawers and found a pile of bank statements. There seemed to be frequent payments to a Mrs Ria Silva – lots of small amounts as well a regular monthly payment of £400 to this woman's account. In another drawer she found receipts for furnishings, jewellery, books and CDs, none of which she'd ever seen in their house. In the bottom drawer were more receipts, mostly from bookmakers and it seemed Raja was a heavy gambler, and a quite successful one at that, if his bank account was anything to go by. The realisation that Raja was leading a double life came to her like a blow to the chest and she felt winded, unable to catch her breath. She slumped on to a chair and tried to compose herself.

She had a passing thought, a small thunderbolt of clarity, that Raja might actually like her dead. Perhaps that's what he hoped for, and why he hadn't tried too hard to persuade her to have the chemotherapy, and now he wouldn't care if the breast cancer had returned. And who was this Ria person, the recipient of all that money – perhaps she was blackmailing him? She hardly allowed herself the thought that he's taken a lover.

Just then a scrap of paper caught Kiri's eye. She recognised the hand-writing of his secretary, who had scribbled a note with a name, address and phone number on it. The name was 'Dr Penny Huxtable' and the address was somewhere in Essex. She copied it out on to another piece of paper which she popped into her apron pocket, ready to hide it away somewhere safe. This was a name she recognised – the name of one of the medical students she'd met in Kandy all those years ago, but had lost touch with. Raja didn't like her having friends and had destroyed her address book in a rage one day just after they'd moved house. So what in heaven's name was he doing with Penny's address on his desk now?

That was enough for one day. She couldn't absorb much more; she felt exhausted by all she had discovered and scared of whatever else she might find. She closed the drawers carefully and checked that the study was exactly as she'd found it, then crept back out into her world – the world of the dining room and the kitchen – locking the study door behind her. She put the key into her apron pocket and checked the address was still safely tucked away there. She went to the kitchen and hid both these treasures in an empty jar in the larder, next to the rainy-day pot. Raja never ventured into the larder – that was a woman's place.

* * *

That evening, of course, there was no clinical meeting, so after work Raja made his way across the road from the hospital to Ria's flat. She'd arrived home just before him, and the lamps were on, making the place feel warm and cosy. A hearty stew was simmering on the stove and an enticing aroma filled the air. Raja sank on to the sofa with a smile and Ria came to him, took off his shoes, and after a soothing foot massage, put on his slippers. To the outside world they'd have looked like a happily married couple – that is if the outside world could see them, but they were always very discreet and the curtains were neatly drawn across. No-one knew they were in there together, and it suited them both that way. Raja was after all a married man, who wanted the world to think he respected his marriage vows. He'd given up paying for sex with tarts years ago. He didn't need them now that he had Ria, whom he sometimes thought of as a second wife. That made him feel better about himself and less of a cheat – after all in some cultures it was normal to have more than one wife. It did make life more expensive this way, but he had plenty of money and he could keep Kiri short to off-set his other expenses.

As for Ria, he sometimes wondered what she got out of this secret affair, but then again she did seem to enjoy the company he provided, and the extra cash, as well as the little treats he bought her. Raja knew nothing about Ria's financial situation. He knew she liked the independence he allowed her, and of course the regular sex, which was oh, so good between them. She let him do things he'd never dream of doing with his inhibited wife. The sensuous, almost animal sounds she made when they made love thrilled him to his core. Kiri had been silent in their love-making since she'd lost the baby. She was silent even when he knew he hurt her and her silence angered him, making him want to hurt her all the more. There was no anger in the noisy sessions with Ria, just an uninhibited, uncontrollable physical response.

Ria had been widowed about ten years ago, at the age of 33, when her husband, Enrico was killed in a tragic road accident on a cliff-top road in Portugal. Enrico had been driving his father's old Citroën, which was poorly maintained and had worn tyres. His heart-broken father had always blamed himself for the accident, and never got over the loss of his dear son. To assuage his guilt, and as some sort of weird compensation, her father-in-law arranged for a generous annuity to be paid to Ria. He was a rigid Catholic and the only condition to the money was that Ria must stay true to her marriage vows and not take another husband – if she did the money would stop. Ria became not wealthy, but comfortably off overnight. She did worry she might not be able to keep her side of the bargain – she might be able to live without a husband, but not without men completely. She took exotic holidays whenever she wanted, and worked part-time because she enjoyed it, not because she needed the salary. It was a sadness to her that she and Enrico had never had children because of his low sperm count, so she exercised her natural tendencies to nurture in her work, caring for her patients, and this satisfied her well enough. She never got too emotionally involved though – that wasn't her style. She switched off her emotions the day Enrico died, and thanked the Lord she didn't now have children to worry about. She only had to care for herself and she could manage that.

Two years after she lost Enrico she came to England and settled into her job as a staff nurse on the gynae wards. In England she didn't seem to miss Enrico as much as she did in Portugal, where her in-laws reminded her of him daily, and watched her every move. She bought herself a neat little flat near the hospital and kept herself to herself. She was choosy in making new friends, usually preferring the company of men to women – they didn't pry as much and respected her privacy. After one or two casual boyfriends, and lots of holiday romances, she met Raja and she found this reserved man unexpectedly endearing, much to the surprise of her one close girl friend, Helena, who was a sister in Casualty.

'What do you see in him?' Helena would ask, and Ria would reply, with a knowing smile, that he had hidden depths.

'Just be careful,' said Helena one day. 'I've heard he can be difficult, and also you don't want to lose your allowance.' Helena was the only person who knew about the in-laws' money – Ria had let it slip one evening on a girls' night out at the local wine bar, but had sworn Helena to secrecy.

'Careful is my middle name. Don't you worry – I can look after myself, and our arrangement suits me, so let that be the end of it,' Ria replied, closing the subject. She'd long since stopped questioning the rights and wrongs of the situation, and was even getting a little blasé.

11

Kiri woke up alone in a quiet house, relieved the night was over. Her bad ear buzzed, as it often did if she slept badly. Overnight she had tossed and turned, disturbed by dreams and nightmares. Images of her mama came to her throughout the lonely night. Mama looked like a skeleton in her dream and was dressed in grey rags. She dragged herself across a wasteland, alone but for a white dove-like bird which she ignored as it hovered over her. In another dream a bonny baby with chubby cheeks, also dressed in rags, floated on a raft made of palm leaves across an empty red sea. The baby didn't cry, but simply gazed up at the moon and twinkling stars in the sky above.

As she shook herself awake, Kiri tried to recall her dreams and wondered why, unless you made a conscious effort to remember, dreams fade from your mind so quickly in the light of day. She wanted to remember this night's dreams, analyse the images, and search for meaning. She found it hard to think of her lost baby and her mama alone in Sri Lanka. She hoped she wasn't alone and the dove was a sign that someone was watching Mama and caring for her in the refugee camp. Perhaps the baby was her baby and it wasn't dead but travelling through a parallel universe, and gazing at the same moon that Kiri gazed up to on clear nights in England. These thoughts brought her a kernel of comfort as she washed and dressed.

The pain in her left armpit was worse than yesterday, and now a burning sensation spread to her arm and upper chest. It hurt to move her arm, but when she lifted it and looked in the bathroom mirror, she saw a red rash spreading across her left side. She avoided deodorant and applied some moisturising cream, hoping it was just where her clothes had rubbed her skin because her blouse had felt uncomfortably tight yesterday.

By evening time when Raja came home, Kiri was looking drawn and her face was pale. She had managed to prepare a simple meal for him, but as she put it on the table for him Raja noticed she was moving her arm stiffly – hiding a grimace of pain.

'What is wrong with you, woman? What's the matter with your arm? You look as if you've had a stroke. Whatever is wrong with you now?'

'I'm alright, I just have a little rash. Perhaps you can look at it for me and bring me some cream from the hospital tomorrow? I think that's all I need,' said Kiri. She rarely asked Raja for anything these days. She rarely made demands of him for fear of setting off one of his moments. That's what she called his moods and angry outbursts – moments. If she thought of them as moments they would pass more quickly.

When she undressed that night she showed him her armpit. The red rash looked angry now and small blisters had appeared in the area. She could hardly lift her arm to show him because of the pain.

'Oh, for goodness sake, you've got shingles,' he blurted out. 'Whatever next? I can see you won't be much use around the house for a while until this settles. I'll see if I can get you some treatment from the hospital tomorrow.' Then he surprised her by going to his study and bringing back a box of painkillers.

In the morning he brought her a cup of tea in bed, and told her to rest for the day; he would have his breakfast at the hospital and see her tonight. With a curt 'goodbye' he marched out, slamming the front door and locking it behind him. The silly man thinks he has locked me in, thought Kiri to herself. He does not realise the lock on the back door is broken, and that I now have a key to the padlock on the back gate. She'd found the padlock key on the same ring as the spare study key.

She liked the thought that she would be able to leave the house more easily now, without the indignity of having to climb out of the side window – when she had the courage to go out, that is.

She certainly felt too unwell to go out that day. Any effort sent a searing pain to her arm, and her upper chest ached. She struggled to the sofa and rested there all day, watching the World News in the hope of a picture or a story from Batticaloa. She very much hoped Raja would be home soon with some stronger painkillers. She hated that she needed his attention.

Raja meanwhile made a trip to the hospital pharmacy, where one of his few men friends, Mohan, was a dispensing technician. Mohan was a Sri Lankan and a Tamil like Raja, and although they hardly ever met outside work, they did occasionally have tea together in the canteen if Ria was not around. Ria was often not around for days at a time, away on her holiday jaunts, or on a cruise, and Raja valued having someone else to talk to. Ria was due to go off on a cruise soon, Raja reminded himself – Ria liked a good cruise.

Mohan liked to talk politics with Raja, even if Raja preferred to talk cricket. Mohan was well versed in the history of the Tamil United Liberation Front, and spoke to Raja about their goal of a 'sovereign socialist state of Tamil Eelam'. Raja was always excited by their talks, agreeing that the Tamils had been discriminated against by the Sinhalese government, but the side-effect of their discussions was a fuelling of Raja's negative feelings about his wife. Mohan was part of a group of Tamils in Manchester who supported the Tamil Tigers in the war of attrition and who sent money to their cause. He was trying to lure Raja into their militant group, in the hope of attracting some generous donations, but Raja was not being drawn in. Raja simply enjoyed their chats as an intellectual exercise – he was much too self-centred to be political or a revolutionary, and anyway he was Indian not Sri Lankan, so their civil war meant little to him. At least Mohan bothered to sit with him unlike the surgeons at the hospital, who didn't seem to like him much. They were usually polite to him but he never felt truly at ease with them as he did with Mohan. Raja didn't know Mohan only liked him because he had money and could be useful to their group.

Mohan came out of the back room of the dispensary to greet Raja at the front desk of the hospital pharmacy.

'What brings you to my patch, Raja? We don't often see you down here. To what do we owe the pleasure?' said the ever-smiling Mohan.

'I could do with your assistance, Mohan. You know of my wife, Kiri? Well she's come out in shingles in her armpit, and we can't get an appointment with our GP for three days,' lied Raja. 'By then it'll be too late for anti-viral therapy. Can I get some from you? Oh, and she needs some stronger analgesia – paracetamol isn't touching her pain. I'm sorry to have to ask you this, but I knew you'd be a good friend and help us.'

'Poor lady,' replied Mohan. 'Shingles can be nasty and the sooner it's treated the better. Sure man, I can give you some acyclovir and co-dydramol, but you'll have to sign for it of course. Be a bit discreet, though, my boss doesn't like us doing favours. It's not as if I'm doing anything wrong, as long as you sign the prescription, it's just that he likes things done by the book and would say you should get an emergency appointment with your GP.'

'That's all very well, Mohan, but how could I get her there at short notice with my work commitments?'

'I know, I understand. I can sort it,' replied the technician.

'Thanks, Mo, you are a true friend and a gentleman,' said

Raja, who borrowed Mohan's pen and wrote out the prescription for a course of acyclovir and a generous supply of the strong painkillers. Mohan raised an eyebrow at the quantity of tablets he requested, but went into the back room and dispensed the prescribed drugs, labelling the boxes carefully in the name of Kiri de Souza. Raja will certainly owe me after this, he thought, as he handed over the packets – funny his wife uses her maiden name, and he doesn't talk about her much.

Raja got home in good time for once, and administered the tablets to his wife, then opened a large tin of chicken soup for their supper. Kiri had never known him be so helpful, and she was grateful. He even did the washing up and sent her to bed early, while he retired to his study. As she dozed she made a mental note to find out more about this Ria woman when she felt better.

The painkillers made Kiri woozy and a little nauseated, but they did help her sleep. Raja urged her to take them regularly till the pain settled. Over the next few days the drug built up in her system and soon she became so drowsy she could hardly eat or drink. Strange thoughts of her damaged homeland drifted through her muddled mind. She fretted about her mother and felt more and more helpless. She became quieter and quieter and slept for hours at a time. Raja quite enjoyed having such a docile wife, and didn't miss having to talk to her at all. He either took his meals in the hospital canteen or with Ria, and just came home to dose Kiri up with her pills and change his clothes.

It started to dawn on Kiri just what was happening. In her half-awake moments she started to believe that Raja was trying to kill her, so instead of swallowing the painkillers she hid them under her pillow till he was gone, and then she flushed them down the loo. Once she avoided the painkillers her mind cleared and she came to her senses. She took the opportunity to have another look in Raja's study and this time she took away a book of stamps and some stationery, with the idea of writing letters to her mother and to Penny Huxtable. At this stage she hadn't worked out what she would write – that would need some thought. She didn't want to worry her mother any more than necessary, but needed so badly to make contact. She wouldn't want to put Penny off by unloading too much on to her, but she also needed someone to help her, and she had a feeling Penny was the one. She made up lots of practice letters in her head until a plan came together.

12

Ria set off on her cruise after a fine dinner and a fond and physical farewell from Raja. Raja felt low at the thought of being stuck at home with Kiri every evening in Ria's absence. But even so he was starting to get irritated with everything being on Ria's terms – he liked to be the one in control and with Ria the power was shifting. Kiri seemed to have rallied – her shingles rash was drying out nicely, the pain seemed less and she'd got her brain back in gear, worst luck, thought Raja. At least she was cooking again and keeping the house tidier, which was something to be thankful for.

Raja had a rare weekend off, and the winter sun was bright in the icy sky. He fancied a drive out into the countryside. At its last service the garage man had told him that the old Mercedes would benefit from some longer runs. Town driving was wearing out the old engine and it needed a good blow out. For once Raja did what he was told and decided to plan a day trip.

Kiri was amazed when he suggested she go with him for a drive. They hadn't been out together, other than for essential shopping, for ages. She was nervous after the painkiller episode and got it into her head that he might try to kill her. She went into the kitchen to get a glass of water before the trip, and took a small kitchen knife out of the drawer. She felt the cold sharp edge of the blade with her thumb and imagined herself slitting the brake lines beneath the Mercedes just as she'd seen someone do on one of her programmes. She imagined digging the blade in between Raja's ribs. She imagined herself slitting her own wrists.

She slipped the knife into her coat pocket then picked up a bag of apples thinking they might need a snack. Raja sat her in the back of the car, and did up her seatbelt as if she were a child rather than his wife. He can't even get it right when he's trying to be nice, she thought. He settled himself in the driver seat, cursing his own seatbelt which was frayed and awkward to fasten. The engine growled its throaty growl as they drove south into Derbyshire. Kiri relaxed back on the soft leather seat, and for a few hours they pretended they were happy. They never ate the apples – didn't even stop for a breath of air or a walk and Kiri didn't know whether to be relieved to be home safe or not.

Kiri noticed the red light flashing on their answering machine. Raja was putting his precious car away in the garage, so she pressed the button and listened to the message,

'This is a message for Ms Kiri de Souza from the breast clinic,' said the anonymous voice. 'We are sorry you missed your appointment this week. We have had trouble reaching you to see if you are alright. We have sent you another appointment in the post. Please phone 747474 if you are unable to keep this next appointment, or if you need to speak to a care advisor.'

Kiri pressed the delete button just in time before Raja came indoors. She went into the kitchen to prepare supper and to think. She had almost forgotten about the biopsy appointment – not that she had any intention of going, but she did hope they were not going to pester her. She didn't want any treatment and she didn't want to speak to Raja about it, and that was that.

After their meal when Raja went to his study, Kiri started to write her letter to Penny:

Dear Penny,

I hope you do not mind me writing to you after all this time. I lost your address when we moved house, in fact I lost my entire address book, but by some lucky chance I have found it again. I hope you are well, and that our dear friend Jean is also well. I am not so good, in fact my life has become very difficult in recent years and I need a friend and perhaps some advice. I know we live far apart these days, but I wonder if we could talk on the phone? I'm afraid I do not have email and my husband might intercept a letter – he does not know I am contacting you. I can answer my phone, which just receives incoming calls, when he is at work. He is always out from Mondays to Fridays between 8am and 6pm. I do hope you will phone me on 01061333557. If a man answers the phone please hang up and try again. I am sorry to make this so complicated, but you will understand when we speak.

I think often about our happy times together in Kandy. I am heartbroken for my country since the tsunami, but I do know my dear mama is alive, so that is something.

I look forward so much to your call,

With best wishes from your old friend,

Kiri de Souza
(Mrs Raja Coomaraswamy)

Kiri reread the letter and was satisfied with her effort. She didn't want to put too much on paper and frighten Penny off, but she did want her letter to express the serious situation she was in. She folded the letter neatly and tucked it into an envelope, on to which she carefully copied Penny's address in Essex. She added a first class stamp, and slid the completed missive under her mattress until tomorrow.

The next morning after Raja's departure, she decided it was time she left the house on her own. Her heart rate increased and her breath tightened at the thought. You silly woman, she said to herself, you know the way to the post box. It is only a short distance down the road. How hard can it be to post a letter? You can do it, you can do it, she repeated, and with that mantra in her head she put on her green woollen coat, fastening the buttons with trembling hands.

Kiri nudged the flimsy lock on the back door, which easily gave way and allowed her out into the cold air of the back garden. The padlock on the back gate was a little rusty, but after a tussle she managed to open it and she was free – deep breath, one foot after another, you can do it, she repeated. She looked around and saw that the pathway to the main road was empty. She set off with small, cautious steps. One step at a time was all it took to get closer and closer to the post box, and soon she was there, standing right in front of it. She shoved her letter into the slot, hoping it was her first step towards freedom.

13

Kiri felt elated by this small achievement. She realised it had been some weeks now since she'd had a full-blown panic attack and that pleased her. The next day she decided that if she could do one letter, she could do another, and she sat down to compose an important letter to Mama, in Sinhalese this time. She needed to mend the rift that had come between them since her marriage.

15 Autumn Avenue
Salford
Greater Manchester
England
Telephone 01061 333557 (daytimes only)

Dearest Mama,

This is your daughter, Kiri. I hope you receive this letter. I know the house has gone, but I have heard that you are alive. My husband telephoned the Emergency enquiries line after the great wave came to Batticaloa and they told him you were safe and in an emergency camp there. I have no address for the place so hope and pray that this letter will find you. Raja says he will send you money, but I do not always trust him to do as he says.

I am sorry I have not written to you for such a long time. My only excuse is that Raja does not make my life easy, and he has cut me off from my family and any friends I once had. He keeps me more as a servant than a wife. I tell you this, not to worry you, but to explain myself, in the hope that you can forgive me for being such a bad daughter.

I have been ill, but I am getting stronger. I have seen the

awful pictures of destruction in our country, and this has made me determined to find a way home. Mama, it may take some time to find the way, but I will not rest until I can step on Sri Lankan soil once more, even if I do so alone and husbandless.

I think of you everyday Mama. I wonder if my two brothers in America have kept in touch and try to help you. I hope and pray that this is so.

Think of me and send me your prayers, Mama, and I promise that one day we will be reunited, and we can mend any broken bridges between us.

I send this with all my love,

Kiribaba xx

She addressed the envelope to:

Mrs Lali de Souza, formerly of 23, Park Road, Batticaloa, Care of St Mary's School, Batticaloa, Sri Lanka.

That was the best she could do for an address. She knew that a first class English stamp would not get her letter to Sri Lanka, so that was her next challenge. She would have to get to the post office to buy the correct stamp. She knew there was a post office near the grocery shop where Raja bought their vegetables. If she could make it to the post box, surely she could go just a little further to the shopping precinct.

Kiri repeated the escape route she'd learned the day before and took with her some coins from the rainy day pot. She kept her breathing calm as she walked down the road, keeping her eyes low in case anyone looked at her. She was thankful there was no queue at the counter when she got to the post office.

'I want this to go Sri Lanka please, first class please,' she spoke so quietly that the counter clerk had to ask her to repeat herself. Kiri turned her good ear to the glass screen which separated them.

'That will be eighty-eight pence thank you,' replied the young woman in a broad Manchester accent.

'And I'll take another supply of stamps for my next letter too, please,' said Kiri more bravely.

She found the right money and watched the woman stick the different coloured stamps and an airmail sticker on to her envelope, before placing it in her post bag. Kiri made a little wish as she turned and said goodbye. She walked slowly home, and locked herself back in the house.

14

When Kiri failed to turn up at the breast clinic for her scan results and biopsy, it sent a flurry of concern through the team. Dr Anne and Ramona had a bad feeling about this, having admitted to each other that Kiri was very hard to get through to. Dr Anne observed that Kiri's reaction to her disease had been odd from the onset. They went to talk to the counsellor and the social worker, and tried to piece together as much as they could about the timid Sri Lankan woman, who rarely smiled and gave so little away about herself. They all knew that she was at high risk of a recurrence having avoided chemotherapy three years ago.

Ramona offered to phone Kiri, but found the phone number on her notes was incorrect. She got through to an insurance office:

'Sorry dearie, wrong number.'

They decided to put a letter in the post and hoped to goodness the address on file was correct – it wasn't.

Mr Rees came into the office as they were debating what else they could do. He went through her file again. Her next of kin was Mr Raja Coomaraswamy, recorded as 'husband' and 'same address'.

'This sounds all wrong,' said Mr Rees. 'How come none of you know anything about a patient who has been under your care for three years? This isn't good enough. I expect my team to support our patients fully, and really get to know them. That might not have been the approach of my predecessor, but that's how I work. I am not happy with this – we'll discuss this further at tomorrow's team meeting.'

With that he marched out, leaving his team feeling worried,

embarrassed and chastised – most of all they were upset with themselves. Two minutes later he rushed back in.

'Let me see those notes again. That name Coomaraswamy sounds familiar. Isn't there a chap at the Royal in Salford called Coomara, a staff grade surgeon on the gastro unit. I wonder... Get me the gastro secretary on the line now!'

'Hello, Mr Harry Rees here from the Christie in Manchester,' he announced to the secretary. 'Do you have a Mr Raja Coomaraswamy in your department?'

'Well, yes Sir,' came the reply, 'but he calls himself Mr Coomara at work.'

'Good, I urgently need to speak to his wife. Can you give me their home phone number?'

'I'm sorry but we're not allowed to give out home phone numbers, Sir. It's against protocol,' said the secretary.

'I don't give a toss about protocol. This could be a matter of life or death, so I suggest you give me the number. Do you know who I am? I am the new breast specialist at the Manchester Breast Centre and I need to speak to Mr Coomara's wife with some urgency.'

'Shall I ask Mr Coomara to call you back, Mr Rees?'

'No, that will not do. There are patient confidentiality issues here and I need to speak to Mrs Coomaraswamy directly. Now – the number please? I'm sorry to sound impatient and I know you are only doing your job, but I fear it is vital that we contact the wife,' replied Mr Rees in a more conciliatory tone.

The poor secretary was starting to feel she had no choice, and in the end put Mr Rees through to her boss, Mr Thompson, who gave him the phone number – 01061 333557. Of course when Ramona tried the number all she got was an answer phone. She was unsure about leaving a message in this delicate situation, but by the weekend when she made a second failed attempt to get an answer, she did just that. If Kiri hadn't contacted them by the next working week, they decided they would send the social worker to make a home visit.

That evening when he got home after a long hard day at work, Harry Rees decided to give Jean Dowland a ring. He had promised to find out about Raja for her, and he had some other things to discuss with her.

'Hello, Jean, It's Harry here, Harry Rees. How's tricks?'

'Oh, hello Harry. All good here thanks. Have you got some information?' replied Jean chirpily.

'Well, I think I may have tracked down your Mr Raja Coomara, and as I thought all is not straightforward with him.' Harry went on to explain what he'd discovered and then, with a request of confidentiality he told Jean about his concerns for Kiri and her health. As a fellow consultant as well as a friend he felt entirely justified in sharing this, and apart from anything else he wanted to explore his own feelings on the case with someone he trusted. He was genuinely worried that his department had let this woman down, even though it was before he had arrived on the scene.

Jean listened sympathetically to his worries, then reiterated that she and Penny were very keen to re-establish contact with Kiri, and help her in any way they could. Harry agreed to give Jean the contact details, but urged caution – rather than wade in like bulls in a china shop.

'Make an action plan and have appropriate back-up in place first,' he said. Then he played his trump card, 'I know what – why don't you and Penny come up to the Breakthrough Breast Cancer Conference that we're hosting at the Christie next week? You must have seen the invitation in the journals, and you could bring your GP chum along as a welcome guest – we still have some spaces for delegates left. It'll look good on both your CPD files, as well as making a nice couple of days away for you in Manchester.'

'What a great idea. I'm due some study leave. If we come up Thursday night I'll only miss one day at work and my research registrar will cover me – he's always offering. I'll call Penny straightaway and confirm our plans in an email. Can you just send me the conference details and some ideas for suitable hotels?'

'Will do – see you next Thursday evening then. Cheerio,' said Harry, then he went to the kitchen to find his supper, which his wife had kept warm for him in the oven. She'd gone to her yoga class, and the kids were doing their homework. He opened a bottle of Merlot to go with his steak and mushroom casserole, and thought how nice it would be to see Jean again. Despite her being a little older than him, he had always rather fancied her – not that he'd ever do anything about it, but it was always fun to flirt.

Jean couldn't wait to phone Penny and invite her to Manchester. Penny jumped at the idea of a few days away. She only worked a half day on Fridays, so could easily get that covered. She never took all her study leave allowance anyway, so the partners couldn't complain – especially as the senior partner was Clive. Clive might well sulk at being left behind in Essex, but he would cope, and someone had to stay and look after the dog and keep an eye on Hettie and Theo. Jean's three were all away of course, so she wouldn't have that problem. Her eldest was at uni somewhere, and the younger two were at boarding school – poor souls, thought Penny.

Emails flew back and forth over the next few days and soon the plan came together with details for their trip up north confirmed. Despite an over-riding concern for Kiri, Penny and Jean were as excited as two school children going away on a school trip for the first time. Their concern for Kiri only increased when later that week Penny's letter from Kiri arrived.

'We're going at just the right time,' Penny told Jean over the phone. 'I'm going to call her this afternoon as she's asked, and don't worry, I won't put my foot in it. I'll go gently and just feel my way at first. I've got a bad feeling about Kiri – she sounds in real trouble.'

15

Penny still hadn't got round to making her call when there was a knock on Kiri's door. No-one ever came to the door, so Kiri was nervous – she kept quiet, hoping that the visitor would give up and go away. It might just be a Jehovah's Witness or a charity collector. The knock came again, this time louder and more forceful. It was followed by a voice calling through the letter box.

'Hello, is anybody there?' called the female voice. 'I'm looking for Kiri. I'm from the hospital and I'm here to help if I can. Can you hear me? My name is Shelley and I'm a social worker. Can I come in and talk to you?'

Kiri's heart was jumping in her chest and thumping against her ribs. She was feeling sick and her breathing felt tight. She didn't know what to do. She wanted to respond, but didn't dare. What if she made things worse? She'd heard stories about social workers, and Raja wouldn't like it at all. Suddenly her breath returned and she made the decision.

'I'm here. I'm Kiri. Thank you.'

Shelley talked to Kiri through the letter box, reassuring the timid listener that she was here to help and that nothing bad was going to happen to her. Eventually Kiri directed Shelley to the back door and let her in. The two women sat at the kitchen table, and talked and talked. Words flowed out of Kiri as if a dam had been opened. She talked as she had never talked before, feeling strangely safe with this kind but strong social worker. Shelley was firm and professional and Kiri suspected she stood for no nonsense.

Shelley listened carefully and let the flow of words pour forth. She heard about Raja, and the baby, and Kiri's mother and Sri Lanka. She heard about the civil unrest and the tsunami, then

Raja's abuse. When the words slowed down Shelley suggested they needed to think about some practicalities. She offered to find Kiri a place in a women's refuge, but Kiri refused this point blank. She convinced Shelley that she could handle Raja if she knew she had some support in the background.

Behind her dark-rimmed glasses, Shelley's eyes became steely as she discussed the biopsy with Kiri and eventually persuaded her to have the procedure done under local anaesthetic. She had reserved a stand-by appointment for next Thursday, which they would now confirm. After that Kiri would be in a position to plan the rest of her life.

Shelley helped Kiri concoct the story she could tell to Raja. She was to say that a letter had arrived from the breast clinic and the new consultant there had reviewed her scans. He had found a suspicious area of shadowing that he thought should be assessed by a biopsy. She had been given an appointment for next Thursday, and would need to stay in hospital for one night. Kiri practised her story before sending Shelley away. The afternoon was drawing on and Raja would be home soon. She would keep things as normal as possible for just a little longer.

Just after Raja got home, the phone rang. He picked it up and answered, but the caller hung up.

'Must have been a wrong number,' he grunted.

Kiri couldn't face an argument or a debate that evening – she was all talked out. She gave him his dinner and kept out of his way by going to bed early.

16

A letter from the breast unit arrived the next morning, confirming her appointment for Thursday. There was no mention of an overnight stay, and Kiri realised then that this was Shelley's way of trying to get her some space and time to sort herself out. She'd never spent a night away from home before, so she knew she'd feel anxious, but she reassured herself that Shelley and the team would look after her now that everything was in the open. She wondered why she hadn't spoken to any of them before. Perhaps she wasn't strong enough in the past, but now she knew the great strength her people in Sri Lanka were showing, it made her own problems seem so small.

Kiri could hardly believe it when Penny rang that afternoon. It was wonderful to hear her familiar voice, which hadn't changed in all those years. Kiri always thought that Penny spoke perfect 'Queen's English' and had learned from her and improved her own pronunciation.

'Hello stranger. It's Penny here. I was so pleased to get your letter. I'm glad your husband passed on my address to you.'

Kiri didn't let on that he hadn't actually passed the address to her. That detail would wait till later.

'Penny, dear Penny, it's you. Thank you so much for phoning me. I'm sorry to have sounded paranoid in my letter, but as I said, I haven't been well. I've had so many problems. I'm not sure I can tell you it all just now, but the awful tsunami has made me think about you and Jean and our time in Sri Lanka, and I just wanted to talk to you again. It's made me realise my life must change, and that I need some friends.'

'Oh, Kiri. I've been thinking about you since the tsunami too. I've watched it all on the news. I think you said your mother is alive, thank goodness for that. Are you going to be able to go over and see her? Is that what you want help with I wonder? You were a bit mysterious in your letter.'

'Yes, that is one of the things I need help with. How did you know? You see it's all rather complicated. I've been ill, I get these panic attacks, I have no money and I have no passport. My husband does not want me to go, so as you can see it is all too complicated. There is more, but I cannot tell you just yet. It would be too much for now. All I need at the moment is to know I have a friend.' Kiri did however go on to explain a little more.

'I'll see what I can come up with and phone you again in a couple of days with some ideas,' promised Penny. 'Do you mind if I share some of this with Jean? We are both your friends. Just stay strong until we meet again.'

'Thank you, dear, dear friend of old,' Kiri's replied.

'I'm glad you didn't say 'old friend' just then. I'm only 49 you know,' laughed Penny, trying to lighten the tone. 'Cheerio, young friend.'

Penny felt very sad when she put the phone down and made a cup of tea. Her young friend, now about 45 she guessed, had lost so much of the verve she'd had at the age of nineteen. She'd obviously had a rotten life and now was worried about her mother and her country as well as her health and her marriage. News pictures from Sri Lanka still looked grim and stories were continuing to come in of lost western tourists as well as local people.

Penny and Jean worked through some ideas on the phone for the next Thursday. They would get passport forms for Kiri to complete, and take a camera with which to take passport photos. Clive would instruct Penny how to get them right – he was good at all things photographic. They would research the cost of flights to Colombo, and trains across the country to Batticaloa. They would buy a mobile phone and set it up for Kiri, so she could speak to them if she needed them. They would buy stamps and stationery so she could write letters, and take some treats for her as well – maybe chocolates and toiletries and some books. They remembered Kiri always loved reading English books.

Harry had told Jean he'd arranged a private room for Kiri next Thursday, and the biopsy would only take twenty minutes or so, so she could rest until they arrived on Thursday evening. On Friday morning, Shelley, the social worker would be in to see her first thing to assess whether it was OK for Kiri to return home. Penny and Jean would then be able to get to the conference without worrying too much. Hospital transport was arranged to collect Kiri at 8.30 in the morning on Thursday, from 15 Autumn Avenue (not 13 as it said in the notes – it took the resourceful Shelley to work that one out). The same car would take her back home, if that's where she wanted to go, on Friday afternoon but a bed in a women's refuge could be found at short notice if necessary. Harry added that they hadn't quite worked out what to do with Raja yet, but he was on to it and was considering the options.

17

Kiri delayed telling Raja about the letter from the hospital as long as possible, but the following evening, when he was in a reasonable mood, and after an extra good evening meal, she decided the time had come.

'Raja, I have some difficult news I need to share with you,' she began gently. 'I have had a letter from the breast clinic in Manchester. They need me to go back next week after all.' She went on with the story she'd rehearsed with Shelley, and it all came out convincingly.

Raja looked taken aback. He tried to persuade her it might not be necessary at first, then back-tracked when he heard the new consultant was involved. He wondered if the new chap had caught on to his identity, and didn't want any trouble at work. If Mr Rees didn't know who he was yet, it wouldn't be long before he found out, so Raja decided to act the concerned husband for a while.

'OK, if that's what you want you must go and get the biopsy,' he announced, 'but I don't think I can come with you. I have a full theatre list that day. You can go in the hospital car, but why do you need to stay the night? That all seems a bit unnecessary to me. Still if the car is booked both ways for you, we can leave it at that. At least it saves me turning out, or paying for a taxi.'

'I think I am ready to face this. Thank you,' responded Kiri with a tremble in her voice. She was trying not to sound as nervous as she felt.

'You could be giving yourself problems you know. What will you do if you need further treatment? You'll never cope with the chemotherapy. Remember that's what put you off last time. Still it's up to you and you must cross that bridge when you come to it,' said Raja starkly.

The decision was made and Kiri was finding it hard to believe how easy it had been telling Raja. She prepared for bed that night planning what she must pack to take with her. She thought her pink night-dress was the nicest, and her slippers would do, even though they were old. She didn't have a toilet bag, but could make do with a small plastic bag she found. She dug out an old holdall from the spare room and beat the dust from it. She looked around the room – this was the spare room she kept ready for visitors who never came. In the early days in the house she had hoped that their child might use this room, and when that hope faded she hoped her mother might one day come to visit them in England. How foolish had been her dreams in those days, she thought.

For the rest of the week Kiri and Raja hardly spoke. On Thursday Raja left early for work as usual, leaving her with a front door key to let herself out and back in. It was one of the few times in recent years that she had held her own front door key. The hospital car arrived promptly at 8.30 and the kindly driver took her into South Manchester. The driver introduced herself as Maggie. Maggie was about 60, with greying hair, and Kiri detected a posh voice. She made small talk along the way, mostly about the weather, and Kiri answered in monosyllables, thinking she actually preferred the stony-faced taxi driver. Maggie, realising her passenger was nervous, didn't ask too many questions, much to Kiri's relief. They made it through the rush hour traffic in good time for Kiri's appointment, and after a quick 'good luck' from the driver, Kiri made her way down the now familiar corridor, with its familiar smells, to the clinic.

Ramona was there to meet her and helped her settle in to her private side-room on the surgical ward. There was some paperwork to do and a consent form to sign. The biopsy would be done in a small theatre next door, under local anaesthetic, and Kiri was assured it would not hurt. She would have a few stitches and a small dressing which they would remove when she returned for results the following Thursday. Ramona would stay with her throughout the procedure, which Mr Rees would do himself. She was first on his list, and he would do the biopsy before going off to a special conference. He had apparently insisted on this, and Ramona told Kiri how privileged she was, because often a more junior colleague would do this sort of thing. Kiri realised she was getting very special treatment, and wondered quite why she deserved it.

The biopsy went smoothly, and Kiri felt remarkably calm throughout, with Ramona holding her hand. In no time she was back in her room with a cup of tea. She was told to rest until the afternoon, when Shelley the social worker might visit. She dozed on and off until late in the afternoon, when she heard a tap on the door. Expecting it to be Shelley, she called out, 'Hello, come in.'

Two grinning faces peeped round the door. Jean and Penny had got away from work early, caught the train to Manchester and arrived in time for tea. Kiri could hardly believe her eyes and it took her a while to recognise them – her two old friends from so long ago.

'Surprise, surprise,' said Penny as the two women walked in, each carrying an overnight bag considerably smarter than Kiri's dusty holdall. 'Can you cope with a couple of visitors? How are you doing, not too sore I hope?'

Penny and Jean greeted Kiri with hugs and kisses on the cheek, and Jean went off to find three cups of tea and some biscuits, while Penny explained to Kiri how they had found her, and the part Mr Rees had played.

'We do hope we haven't gone too far and that we aren't intruding, but you did say in your letter you needed help. We just felt we were the ones chosen to do the helping.'

'I can't believe you are here,' replied Kiri, who found herself crying with large, slow tears seeping from her dark brown eyes and plopping on to her pink nightie. 'I do need help so very much and now is the right time to accept it. I must get back home to Sri Lanka. Thank you both so much for coming.'

Over tea and biscuits the three women exchanged news, but there was almost too much to say. Jean interrupted the conversation and reminded them that there would be plenty of time for catching up, but the main priority was to get Kiri well, strong enough to deal with Raja, and to get back to Sri Lanka.

Just at the right time, Shelley came to join the discussion. It was decided that Shelley would accompany Kiri home the next day, and stay with her until Raja appeared after work. Jean and Penny would attend their conference and then take a taxi across the city to Autumn Avenue, aiming to be there when Raja arrived home at about 6 o'clock. All four women would face him together.

18

That evening over a sumptuous dinner at their four-star hotel, Penny and Jean talked some more, and tried the set the world to rights. After dinner their thoughts returned to good times in Sri Lanka, finding more forgotten memories of 1978. Penny explained that Clive had always gently resisted her plan to go back to Sri Lanka – he'd never been attracted to anywhere east of the Mediterranean. Anyway the children had come along, and their careers had taken over their lives. When finally they had both time and money the communal troubles had set in and the civil war between the Tamils and the Sinhalese was disrupting tourism, so a visit was never possible.

Jean reminded Penny she had managed a return trip with Daniel for their eighteenth wedding anniversary in 1999. She'd sent her a post card with a picture of a parading elephant on it. They'd left the children in her sister's care and had a romantic second honeymoon. They visited Anuradhapura, but never found Ronni and Bernie's house. They visited the temples of Polonnaruwa and the rock caves of Dambulla. They climbed the wonderful fortress of Sigiriya and Jean showed Daniel the beautiful terraces and wall paintings of mysterious ladies. They went on safari in Wilpattu and stayed there overnight in the resthouse so they could see the sunrise and the early morning wildlife. Daniel was as captivated by it all as Jean had been. Penny couldn't help but be envious.

'We should go back again, Jean – maybe when the fighting settles, or do you think we might need to go sooner, with Kiri?' said Penny.

'Do you know, I think that might be the answer,' said Jean. 'It'll be easier for Kiri to travel with friends, won't it? So that's what we could do.'

They finally stopped talking and fell asleep in their twin beds, dreaming of Sri Lankan spices and heat, and palm trees lining beaches along tropical seashores, whilst hoping it would rise again from the damage of the tsunami.

Penny and Jean treated themselves to a full English breakfast, and then took a taxi to the Holt Theatre, at the Paterson Institute of Cancer Research, for the conference. Penny loved being in the academic setting again. She always enjoyed attending study courses as a GP, updating her knowledge and exercising her brain in new ways. She soaked up all the lectures and made notes on how to enhance her own practice. She watched Jean absorb it all too, asking pertinent questions of her peers. It was like being back at university, only better. They enjoyed a buffet lunch and chatted to the other delegates, then returned for the afternoon session during which Harry Rees gave an excellent talk on new diagnostic techniques. Listening to a good and fluent speaker was always rewarding, thought Penny, and he was easy on the eye too.

At the end of the day they caught up with Harry and the conversation came round to Kiri. Harry was hopeful that her biopsy would show simple scar tissue, but said they must wait for the full report from Histology. They were all to keep their fingers crossed.

So with fingers and toes crossed Penny and Jean made their way to Salford for the 6 o'clock meeting. Shelley was already there and made cups of tea for them while they waited for Raja. They helped fill out the passport form, and Penny took photographs of Kiri, which she could countersign to confirm her identity, after which she hoped the fast track facility at the post office would ensure a quick return. This was to be the next step in getting Kiri back to her homeland. They presented Kiri with a new mobile phone and a rape alarm, and showed her how to use the new devices to keep herself safe.

All these things were carefully hidden away by the time Raja's car engine throbbed in to the drive. When he walked through the front door his face turned ashen, and then puce.

'What on earth is going on here, Kiri? Who are these people, and who let them into our home?' Raja sounded angry.

The three visitors introduced themselves simply as Kiri's friends. He thought she had no friends and looked suspiciously at Penny, Jean and Shelley in turn. He could tell they were determined and confident women, who meant business.

'And what may I ask are you all doing here this evening? My wife is not well. She has had an operation and I don't think she needs visitors tonight. I would like you to please leave her alone.'

Shelley was the one to respond. 'I don't think we can just leave her alone, Mr Coomaraswamy. As well as being Kiri's friend, I am a social worker and I work for the Manchester Breast Unit with her new consultant, Mr Harry Rees. We are all very concerned about Kiri's care. Penny and Jean are both doctors. You may remember them from the old days in Kandy in Sri Lanka?'

It all fell into place as Raja glared at Penny. This was the woman who had tried to contact him at work.

'You!' was all he could manage to utter before Shelley continued.

'Mr Coomaraswamy, or perhaps I can call you Raja? We know all about what has happened to Kiri since she came to England, and I do mean *all* that has happened.' Shelley sounded firm, but calm and considerate. She didn't want to stir Raja's anger any more than she had to, and was keen to keep the lines of communication open with him.

'We know how difficult life has been for you both, but our

concern is for Kiri. It is so important she gets the care she needs for her breast cancer. As a surgeon yourself I'm sure you understand this.'

'She doesn't want any treatment. It is well documented that she refused chemotherapy three years ago. She wouldn't be able to cope, so that's that. Perhaps you will leave now, and allow me to look after my wife?' Raja was sounding less sure of himself now that he realised the women knew who he was, and where he worked.

'Things have changed, Raja,' it was Jean who chipped in now. 'Kiri has contacted Penny and asked for help. She feels strong enough to face up to her condition if we all help her. She wants to be well enough to go back to Sri Lanka to see her mother, and why on earth should she not be able to?'

'But, but...' stammered Raja.

Jean pressed on. 'We would like to help renew her passport, and get her fit to travel. If she needs travelling companions Penny and I will accompany her. It need not put you out at all.'

'We cannot afford it, so you can forget that suggestion,' blurted Raja, who'd found his second wind. 'It's time for you to go now, but I will get her to the breast clinic next week if that's what she wants.'

Now it was Penny's turn to speak up, 'Raja, we will get Kiri to Sri Lanka if it's the last thing we do, and even if it takes some time. I'm sure we can come to some arrangement about the airfare, and I don't think you will be in a position to stop us.'

'Don't you threaten me. Now get out of my house and stop meddling with things that don't concern you.' Raja was beginning to raise his voice and his anger was visible.

Jean calmly took control and played the winning card.

'We know that you have made our friend's life a misery,

abused her, hit her and knocked the self-esteem out of her. You have dashed her confidence and treated her like a servant. If you obstruct us then all this will come out. Your colleagues at the Royal will find out and I suspect they will make *your* life a misery. That is, if we don't call the police and have you prosecuted. Between us we have enough evidence for that.'

Raja's working life at the Royal wasn't great, but he couldn't face the humiliation of exposure, and what would Ria say if he was known as a violent wife beater? He would lose her and the comfort she gave him. Raja decided to play it their way for now. He might have to deal with Kiri after they'd gone.

As if she'd read his mind Shelley spoke up,

'And if you think you can play your usual tricks and get at Kiri tonight or hurt her in any way, I can assure you we will involve the police. If you harm a woman on the day after a surgical procedure I can guarantee we'll get you struck from the Medical Register. We have given Kiri a mobile phone with all our numbers on it, as well as a direct line to the Domestic Violence Unit at the police station. She also has a rape alarm – a very loud rape alarm. Kiri will phone me at bedtime and if she has not phoned me by 11 o'clock tonight I will send the domestic violence team round. Kiri and I will keep in touch over the weekend and I will visit again on Monday. I suggest you keep your head down until she returns to the clinic next Thursday for her results. A hospital car will be booked for Thursday morning.'

'Is that it? Is that what you want, Kiri? You haven't said a word,' said Raja who turned to his wife. 'If I agree to this, will that be all?'

'That's it for now,' said Shelley. 'Kiri is happy with all this – isn't that right Kiri?'

Kiri nodded as Shelley continued,

'The rest depends on you, Raja, and how you behave from now on. It might be in your best interest to work with us on this. Do not try to block us.'

'That sounds like a threat,' responded Raja.

'Just try me,' replied Shelley. She then slipped away giving Kiri a little wink as she left.

Raja retired quickly to his study and poured himself a large whiskey. He made no further appearances that night, and slept fitfully on the couch in his study. Penny made Kiri scrambled eggs for her supper and she and Jean helped Kiri to bed after reinforcing Shelley's instructions. They had to get the train back to London early the following morning, but said they would phone regularly. Penny promised she would drive up to Manchester as soon as she could after the histology results were known. Kiri assured them she felt well enough to be left and after hugs all round, she let her friends leave.

Back at the hotel Penny and Jean treated themselves to a bottle of fine wine, and with sighs of relief they raised their glasses to Kiri's health. They were pleased Raja hadn't kicked off, but acknowledged that Kiri's problems were not necessarily over.

'I told you he was a creep. I think she might benefit from some counselling for the panic attacks if nothing else, don't you?' said Jean.

'Yes. I was wondering if we should have asked Shelley to arrange something for her – some decent talking therapy might help, or even CBT if it's available. I'll mention it when we know the biopsy results,' replied Penny.

Before they collapsed into bed, exhausted by the day's activities, Jean remembered to email Harry. He'd been waiting for their message and replied straightaway, phoning Jean on her mobile to say well done. He was chatty after a nice evening in the hospital bar in Manchester at the end of the conference. He'd met some of the Salford consultants and their guests who turned up and he befriended one of the GI surgeons, a Mr Ellis, and a gynaecologist called Mr Morris.

'They could be useful contacts,' he commented. 'Morris seemed a good chap – he had a very nice woman with him, a nurse called Ria as I recall. Odd really, 'cos I'd heard he was married to a physio. I must have got it wrong. Anyway – have a good journey home and keep in touch.'

19

Kiri and Raja somehow managed to get through the next few days by avoiding each other as much as possible. Kiri sewed and watched television and Raja hid away in his study. Kiri didn't care if he was gambling or internet dating for that matter, just as long as he kept away from her. Shelley's phone calls did a great job in reassuring her and keeping her positive about the future. The thought of the biopsy result hung over her like a threatening thunder-cloud, which she tried to push away if it loomed too close. There was little else she could do until Thursday, so she sewed and sewed, until her finger tips stung.

On Tuesday Raja announced he might be late home from work and he muttered something incoherent about a meeting.

'You can eat alone tonight and have some of the peace you desire,' were his parting words. He hadn't even mentioned the biopsy since Friday, or asked if her wound was alright, but then what did she expect? Peace was still a long way off, thought Kiri.

After work Raja had it in mind to surprise Ria, who he thought was due back from her cruise that afternoon. They had arranged to see each other on Wednesday night when he was next on call, but he couldn't wait. He needed to talk to someone or else he might explode and there was no-one he could tell about Kiri and his problems with her apart from Ria. Ria didn't know the extent of their marital disharmony and certainly knew nothing of the abuse he hurled upon Kiri, but she did know the couple had significant problems and that Kiri had suffered from cancer. To off-load a limited and censored version of last week's events would be easy enough and might bring him some relief.

He felt a shiver of excitement as he walked across the road towards her flat. On the pavement he passed Mr Morris, the gynaecologist, who was striding along in the opposite direction. The two men acknowledged each other with a nod and kept on walking. Raja knocked at the door which Ria opened with an open smile. The smile quickly changed to a questioning frown when she saw who was on her doorstep.

'What in heaven's name are you doing here? I thought you were coming tomorrow, or Wednesday,' she said, sounding tired and weary.

'I know,' said Raja, 'but I really wanted to see you and talk to you. I know you are only just back and I won't stay long if you're tired, but can I come in for a quick drink and a chat?'

Ria recovered her composure and invited him in. She gave him a hug and sat him down on the sofa while she put the kettle on.

'Mmm, new perfume – nice. Is it from Duty Free?' he asked. 'I'll just use your bathroom if I may?'

On the way to the bathroom he glanced into the bedroom. There was no sign of a suitcase. She must have unpacked quickly he thought. She was always so tidy and he did like a tidy house.

'How was your cruise?' he asked when she brought in the tea tray with some chocolate cookies on a plate. 'There obviously wasn't much sun. You've not picked up much colour.'

'Oh it was fine,' she replied. 'Very relaxing – not sunny, but I didn't mind. There was plenty to do on board and I enjoyed reading my books. But tell me why you have come to see me so urgently? You seem edgy. Is something wrong? Is it Kiri? Has she found out about us? Is that it? I knew she might find out one day and that might be the end of our times together. Tell me. Tell me what's happened.' Ria was starting to sound edgy too.

Raja took a deep breath and gave his edited account of the week's events, focussing on the letter from the breast clinic and the biopsy. He admitted that his main concern was Kiri's desire to return to Sri Lanka, and he was worried that she meant to return for ever, not just a holiday. He told her he didn't want to go back to Sri Lanka or to India – not even for a visit. He told her it would look like professional failure and he had no wish to return with his tail between his legs. What use would a holiday be in a country in crisis? It would be a waste of time and money and would be all too complicated. 'And I would miss you,' he added.

'Poor Kiri,' said Ria. 'You should consider her wishes you know. I can see you are in a tricky situation. Don't make any quick decisions – I think you should keep your mind open. I would miss you too of course.'

She yawned. 'I'm rather tired from my journey. Do you mind going soon? We can talk more tomorrow, but that's enough for now. Give me a ring when you're coming over on Wednesday evening.'

Raja walked back to the hospital car park in a quite different mood. He wended his way home to his grey house, in the grey street, to his grey wife, on a misty grey evening in Salford. He did wonder what he was doing here after all, but his family had disinherited him after the splitting-up from Charmina, so there was no point going back to India. He had few friends in Sri Lanka where he had always felt like an outsider so he would be no happier there than in England. He felt he was a lost soul whichever continent he inhabited.

Two days later he was on call. He liked to go over to Ria's place at about 11 p.m. if all was quiet on the surgical wards. During the evening he would catch up with letters and paperwork, as long as he had a good registrar on duty with him, and maybe watch some television in the doctors' lounge first. There was no point in leaving the hospital premises too early, just to risk being called back by an untimely bleep. He usually phoned Ria when he was on his way – she seemed to like some warning of his arrival, especially if it was early.

That Wednesday evening the emergency admissions were bizarrely quiet, and his paperwork was all up to date. He was just about to call Ria to announce an early turn when his bleeper went off. The junior houseman had a query about some unusual lab results which Raja easily settled over the phone, but the matter distracted him and he forgot to make his call to Ria. He trotted across the road to her flat and entered the downstairs lobby. As he climbed the stairs to the second floor apartment the doors of the lift opened and out swished Mr Morris. Morris hastily exited the front door, leaving a waft of strong aftershave behind him. The smell seemed familiar – rather like Ria's new perfume he thought.

Ria looked flushed when she opened her door.

'You're very early,' she said. 'Quiet night? Come on in.'

She gave him a peck on the cheek and once more he smelled that perfume, only it wasn't perfume – it was a man's aftershave.

'I've just seen that Morris fellow in the lift,' he said. 'Was he up here seeing you?'

'Yes. He was just dropping off some papers for work. He wants me to do some extra shifts on his ward,' she replied.

'I bet he does,' said Raja, and with that he raised his right hand and struck her across the side of her face. Ria gasped and twisted backwards, knocking her right eye against the corner of the bookcase in the hall. As she stumbled to the floor she felt a kick beneath her ribs. She was momentarily winded, then screamed at the top of her voice, 'Get out. Get out of my house, and don't ever come back. Go. Get out. Now!'

Raja slumped to his knees weeping, 'I'm so sorry,' he sobbed. 'I don't know what came over me. I thought you were seeing someone else, and I need you, Ria. I need you and no-one else can have you.'

'Shut up, you pathetic little man, and get out before I call the police. Is that what you want, eh? Well get out and I might just do that anyway.'

Ria clutched the side of her face. She felt blood drip through her fingers and rushed to the bathroom. She bathed her face, and in the mirror saw a bruise already appearing under her right eye. The blood was coming from a graze on her cheek where Raja's ring, like the claw of a wild animal, had caught her skin. She reached up to the bathroom cupboard to find cotton wool, and her right side felt sore and bruised. No-one does this to Ria Silva, she thought.

Raja left and walked in the cold air outside, gathering his thoughts before he could risk returning to the hospital. Ria realised she needed photographic evidence of her injuries while fresh, and dialled 999. The Domestic Violence Unit had officers in the area so responded remarkably quickly. They escorted Ria to Accident and Emergency to get her injuries checked and documented, then took a statement while they all waited for Raja to return. Ria's friend Helena was duty Casualty sister that night, and she had bleeped Raja as soon as she saw her friend's face. Ria had been a little vague on details, but Helena had read the signs. She hoped Ria was giving the police more information, because she was convinced Raja had hit her. Of course Raja had chosen the wrong woman – Ria wouldn't let him get away with this sort of behaviour. She would take him to the cleaners, thought Helena.

When Raja returned to the hospital, in response to his bleep, he was most surprised to find two police officers waiting for him – a sharp-looking young WPC and her gangling male colleague. They asked him to accompany them to the station to answer some questions about an attack that night on a Mrs Ria Silva.

'What attack? What nonsense is this?' bluffed Raja. 'I popped over to see her earlier this evening and she was fine when I left. She must have fallen and hit her head.'

'Who said anything about a head injury, Mr Coomara? I think you'd better come with us. Sister has arranged for the registrar to cover your work, and he will call the head of department if he needs advice. I would advise you not to say anything else until we get to the station to take a formal statement.'

'Tell me first, how is Ria?' asked Raja. 'What is happening with her? She is OK, isn't she?'

'I'll just tell you she has to stay in overnight for observation. You seem very worried, Mr Coomara. I wonder why so worried,' said the young police woman.

'She is my friend. Of course I am worried.'

As they led Raja to the waiting police car Helena heard Raja say that he wanted a solicitor present, and she allowed herself a little smirk when she heard the policeman's reply, 'I think you've been watching too many crime dramas on TV, Sir.'

20

Raja spent a miserable night at the police station. He refused to answer any questions until a duty solicitor was found. He told the solicitor that Ria had fainted and injured herself by falling against a book case in the hall, landing across a shoe rack. He denied hitting the woman and assured him that she was fine when he left her. The police recorded his statement and he was released early the next morning, with instructions to return the following afternoon. He took a taxi back to the hospital car park, then drove out of town, beneath heavy snow filled clouds, to look for a transport cafe for breakfast. Here he worked out what he would do next.

He drove home and surprised Kiri with his early return. He told her he was unwell and she would have to go alone to the clinic for her results. Kiri hadn't expected him to go with her and he certainly didn't look good, so she set off as usual in the hospital car. Raja went to his study and wrote a letter to the registrar, Jack, thanking him for covering the night before. He asked him to kindly not discuss last night's events with anyone, at least not until he'd had time to come in to talk to Mr Thompson, the senior consultant. He emailed the letter before 9 o'clock when he phoned the departmental secretary.

'Hello Angie. It's Raja Coomara here. I cannot work today. I am ill, but I do need to speak to Mr Thompson urgently. When will he be available?'

'I'm expecting him in the office at about eleven, after his private clinic. Shall I call him on his mobile?' asked Angie.

'No, don't worry – I'll come in and see him personally. I expect he'll be in the office for the rest of the morning. Can you pencil me in his diary please?' asked Raja.

Angie thought he sounded awful.

'Well, if you're not too poorly, I guess I can do that. Are you sure?' she replied.

'I'm sure. See you at eleven, and don't worry – it's nothing contagious.'

Meanwhile Ria was taken for a scan of her kidney. She was back in her bed when the Casualty doctor came to see her.

'You've been lucky, Mrs Silva,' he told her. 'Your scan looks fine and your urine has tested clear for blood, so if you feel up to it you can go home – that is after the police have been back to speak to you. Just take it easy for a few days and I think you should have at least a week off work after last night's trauma.'

'Thanks. I will,' agreed Ria.

Her head still ached and she'd had a restless night on the noisy assessment ward. She'd had time to consider and decided not to press charges after all. If she did her dalliance with Mr Morris would become public knowledge and she couldn't face the backlash. It would ruin his life, and her job, and just wasn't worth the aggravation. It might also jeopardise her annuity from Enrico's father and that would really restrict her. The decision was made – she would stop seeing Mr Morris, as well as finishing things with Raja. She would just keep her head down at work while the dust settled, then all would be well.

She told the police that her mind had cleared and she thought she must have fainted a second time and fallen badly after Raja had left. The bump on her head had confused her. She'd changed her mind and no longer wanted to press any charges. The WPC was astonished at this change of heart.

'Are you sure? If he hurt you, you can't want him to get away with it. You seemed so certain last night. What if he attacks more women? Surely you owe it to others to get him prosecuted. If you are afraid of him we can protect you.'

'No. I'm not afraid,' Ria insisted. 'Last night I was confused, but now I'm sure it was a silly accident. You cannot persuade me to say otherwise, and my mind is made up. That's the end of the matter, thank you. I can look after myself, so can I go home now and get some proper rest?'

'If that's how you want to play it, we can't stop you,' said the WPC, 'but here, take my card and if you change your mind or need further help don't hesitate to contact me. Goodbye, Mrs Silva, and take care.'

As the police officers left, Ria heard the gangly policeman comment that at least that meant less paperwork – his female colleague gave him a withering look. Ria left shortly after the police, just missing Raja as he was finding a space in the doctors' car park. From home she telephoned a locksmith and arranged to have her locks changed on the front door and to have a peephole fitted. He said he would bring an alarm system with him to demonstrate to her – she'd been thinking of having one for some time, and now she would jolly well get on with it.

Before she settled down for a rest she sent a discreet but firm text to Mr Morris's mobile saying she would not see him again. She gave no explanation, and suggested they simply remain professional if their paths crossed at work. She sent an email to her nursing officer asking for a transfer to a different department when she returned from a week's sick leave, saying she'd had an accident and would send a sick note through the post. She explained she needed a change from gynaecology and would like a spell in outpatients if that could be arranged. Jobs done, she could now rest. When she closed her eyes, flashbacks of Raja's angry assault disturbed her dozing. Although her face looked bad, it was the aggression of that kick that exposed the truth of the man. The memory of it made her shudder and she tucked a blanket firmly round her shoulders.

* * *

Raja could not rest either. He needed to get some control back. He managed to shave and shower, and after a change of clothes he felt more human and ready to face Mr Thompson. He sat outside the office waiting for Mr Thompson to finish a phone call. His own mobile phone startled him. It was his solicitor – Ria had dropped all charges. She had changed her story to the police, saying that the whole thing was a mistake and she had fainted. Raja just needed to call in to see him that afternoon to tidy things up, and the matter was over. Raja felt a wave of relief pass through him, and was looking puzzled and bemused when Mr Thompson called him in.

'What's going on, Raja?' asked Mr Thompson in a concerned voice. He was known to be a firm but fair boss – a decent man, and Raja decided he needed to confide in him in order to survive.

'Thank you for seeing me at such short notice. I had some problems last night and had to leave my post. I want to apologise most sincerely and assure you it will not happen again,' blurted Raja.

'I heard there was a problem. Now I think I need an explanation before we decide what action to take, don't you agree? It is out of order to leave a registrar in charge and unsupported without at least informing another senior member of the department. It's lucky for all concerned that it was a quiet night. I gather Jack and the houseman only had to do a couple of appendicectomies, and explore a superficial knife wound, so you were lucky. I know Jack is one of our more capable registrars, but I remain unimpressed with your dereliction of duty, so fill me in. What happened to you?' asked Thompson.

Raja had to change tack in the light of the call from the solicitor, but still needed to provide an explanation for his absence:

'I was feeling ill. I have not slept well recently because I am so worried about my wife. As you know she had breast cancer three years ago and now she has some symptoms suggestive of a recurrence. She is having investigations, but being such a timid woman she is not coping well and it is affecting us both. I felt I needed to talk to someone about it so went to have a cup of tea with my friend who lives near the hospital. The wards were quiet and I was within bleep range, so I didn't tell Jack I was going. The trouble is that my friend had a fall getting up too quickly to open the door. She hit her head and it made her confused. I took her to the Accident and Emergency department and somehow they got the idea that I had beaten her up. They called the police and I was taken to the police station. It was awful, simply awful. They kept me there all night, and this morning I was so distressed I needed to go home to my wife. I couldn't work, I was just too exhausted.'

'What a dreadful tale. How ghastly for you,' said Mr Thompson. 'How is your friend now, and of course your poor wife? Dear me, Raja, you should have come to me sooner to say you were struggling. I'm sure we could have helped avoid all this mess.'

Raja pressed on with his deceit. 'My wife likes to keep things very private. She doesn't want people feeling sorry for her. She has always been of a nervous disposition and likes to stay at home, keeping herself to herself. That's why she never comes to social events at the hospital. That's why I have found the situation so difficult to handle. She has few friends of her own to share it with.'

'You poor fellow – what a strain it must be for you. Still you should have told me this sooner. I'm glad you had your friend to talk to. How is your friend after the fall?'

'She's fine, thank you, just a little shaken by the accident. She has cleared it with the police now that she is feeling better. They have of course apologised to me for the misunderstanding. I must agree the strain has been considerable with my poor Kiri's problems. My friend was a nursing colleague who was good to talk to. It has helped no end to have a woman's view of such matters.'

'Yes, I'm sure. Thank you, Raja for being so open with me. I think no harm has been done by your actions last night and I can understand how you were feeling. You know, you never take all of your annual leave – I think we should send you off for a couple of weeks to get some rest and relaxation and spend time with your wife. Yes, that's it – you take the next two weeks off as leave and return hopefully refreshed and more able to cope after that. If there are problems in the meantime I want you to phone me personally. OK?'

'Thank you so much. Time off is just what I need. Thank you for your understanding.'

Phew, that went well, thought Raja as he walked downstairs to catch Jack for a word on his way out. He gave Jack the same story about Ria being a supportive friend and her confusion after an awkward faint and fall. Jack looked unconvinced but thought he'd keep quiet for now at least, so nodded and tried to look sympathetic. Jack was pleased Raja would be taking two weeks off – he had no intention of becoming this man's ally, and it would give him a chance to catch up with Helena and maybe even Ria to get their side of the story.

Raja didn't feel like going home and there was no way he wanted to join Kiri at her appointment so he set off in his Mercedes for a therapeutic drive. It was a cold wintery day but the clouds looked less threatening so he made for Heaton Park and stopped for a walk. He found a cafe there and warmed himself with soup and crusty bread. He started to plan his time off. He would give himself some trips to the betting shop rather than gamble on line. He would take walks and work off some of the middle age spread that was settling round his waist. He would have outings and explore the local area – he might even take Kiri for a drive again one day, if she would go. Stupid woman would probably refuse, he thought, now she was starting to stand up for herself. He had a feeling her new-found confidence would cause trouble. It might be nicer to take Ria out, but he suspected he'd burned his boats with her. If she did give him the push, he still had the cards and numbers of those escort girls he used to visit, hidden away somewhere in his study desk.

21

Kiri's day was almost as demanding on the nerves as her husband's had been. As soon as she arrived in clinic, Dr Anne and Mr Rees were called away to an emergency and Kiri had to wait in the waiting area for almost an hour, getting more and more nervous as each minute passed. Shelley was busy in her office with another client and Ramona was rushed off her feet trying to calm all the waiting women. She gazed at the other women and it dawned on her that she wasn't the only one, and every one of these patients was no doubt facing her own demons. She was fidgety and tried to distract herself by reading the posters and notices on the wall, describing all the different types of support available if you had concerns about breast cancer. Kiri couldn't think why she hadn't read them before, and why her eyes and mind had been closed to offers of help in the past. Fear was the only excuse she could find. Now she was still full of fear but that fear had a strand of hope running through it.

She read a poster about the counselling services available through the clinic. She seemed to remember this was something Penny was keen on, but she wasn't sure it was for her. She was slightly more interested in a poster about a self help group, based at the community centre near her home in Salford. They held a coffee morning on the second Wednesday of every month, when they raised money for the Breakthrough Breast Cancer charity. Sometimes they had guest speakers or activity days. She'd heard Jean talk about this charity and it was her involvement with it at a national level that encouraged Kiri to take more interest. She carefully jotted down the phone number of the organiser, and details of the local group. As she looked up from her notebook her eyes met those of another waiting woman. They exchanged shy glances and Kiri noticed that the other woman had no eyelashes and no eyebrows. She was still very attractive but there was an unhealthy pallor to her fair skin. The woman had large blue eyes which looked watery – not through tears, but through a delicate luminosity of internal colour. Her head was covered by an elaborately arranged cotton scarf, printed in green, red and gold. It reminded Kiri of her country's flag and she found herself staring at it. The pale woman caught her eye again and Kiri said 'Sorry', thinking she had caused offence.

'Don't worry,' replied the woman, 'I just saw you looking at that poster. I go to that group but I've not seen you there. Are you interested?'

'It is near my house, but I really don't go out much. I don't know,' replied Kiri casting her eyes down to the lino floor.

Ramona appeared and whisked Kiri away and into the doctor's consulting room. Dr Anne sat next to Mr Rees, behind the desk.

'I'm so sorry we've kept you waiting, Kiri. May I call you Kiri? Let's get to the point. We have your results back from the lab and we're very pleased. We can see no evidence of malignant cells in the sample – that means no cancer,' said Mr Rees with a wide smile. 'We would like to examine you once more before you escape. Ramona, please could you take Kiri to the examination room, and remove her stitches so we can have a good feel? Thanks.'

It stung having the stitches out, but Kiri didn't mind at all – her result was negative and that's all that mattered. The two doctors came in and made their examination and rechecked her scans. Once satisfied that all was well they invited Kiri to dress and then join them back in the consulting room.

'Everything seems to be fine, Kiri. That area of thickening

is much smaller and with the negative biopsy I think we can be happy. I imagine we were feeling a lymph node which had swollen in reaction to the developing shingles, but we had to be certain. Now, I know you didn't want chemotherapy in 2001, and it seems you have got away with it, but I would now recommend some treatment with some tablets, to really reduce the risk of your cancer recurring,' explained Mr Rees.

'What would that involve and how long for?' asked Kiri.

'I would suggest you took them for about two years initially and it would just be one tablet a day. I'm not going to pretend this treatment is totally free from side-effects, but the evidence is that the advantages significantly outweigh the disadvantages. I'm going to ask Dr Anne to go through the precise details with you, then I'll pop back before you leave the clinic. We will want to see you again in three months time to keep an eye on things whatever you decide. Is that OK?'

After a long talk with Dr Anne, Kiri decided to give the tablets a go. Ramona walked round to the hospital pharmacy with her to get the prescription dispensed, then they went back to see Shelley, the social worker. Shelley had Kiri's notes in front of her.

'I'm so glad you have had good results. It's excellent news. Now you can get on with planning what to do next, and deciding how to deal with that husband of yours. Have you thought any more about getting the police involved?'

'I have thought long and hard,' replied Kiri, 'but no – it would end up as his word against mine, and he can be very manipulative. I think it would make things worse.'

'Kiri, you cannot go on like this – surely you are putting your head in the sand,' said Shelley. 'I have been trying to fix up some counselling for you – you know some talking therapy. What would you think to that?'

'How would that help? I now have friends to help me and talk to. I know I must make changes and I will. I don't want anyone else involved. No counsellor, thank you.'

Shelley sighed, 'If you say so, but tell me if you change your mind.'

'I will, but you'll be pleased to know I am making some plans in my mind already,' said Kiri, with pride.

'What sort of plans?'

'I'm going to leave him. I will leave England too and return to Sri Lanka. I don't care if I'll have no money, as long as I can get home. I think with my small savings, and a little help from Penny and Jean, I might be able to manage a one way flight, and that is all I'll need. I don't know how long it will take to arrange this, but it will happen. I will go, and Raja can – how do you put it – 'stew in his own juices'? If he tries to stop me or to make my life awful in the meantime, I will tell the world about his behaviour. I have nothing to hide. He does not need me and I do not need him. I think now he will let me go,' Kiri said, with an authority that surprised Shelley.

'Wow. Good for you,' she replied. 'But if things get tough again you must phone me and ask for help, or phone Penny or Jean, or Ramona or Dr Anne – any of us. We don't want you to slip backwards. Oh, here's Mr Rees to say goodbye.'

'Now remember Kiri, we do need to see you in three months' time for review. Will that be alright?' he asked.

'What if I'm not here?' said Kiri.

'What do you mean, not here?' asked Mr Rees. For a moment he thought she must have misunderstood the good news he had just delivered.

'I want to return to Batticaloa, where I was born. It'll probably take me more than three months to get back there but that is my aim.'

'OK, fine. Good for you. If you do suddenly go please give us a contact address and we can provide you with a letter of introduction to a breast specialist in Sri Lanka. There are good teams in Colombo and Kandy, but I must say I don't know much about Batticaloa. We can check that out. I think it has a university hospital so should be fine. We would like you to remain under surveillance and I'm sure they can do that. Anyway, I'll say goodbye for now, and take care. Ramona will help you with your follow-up appointment and you have your tablets, which I'm delighted you've agreed to take.'

Kiri left the department to go and find her driver to take her home. In the corridor she saw the fair lady waiting for her.

'I realise I should have introduced myself,' she said, holding out her hand to Kiri.

'My name is Pauline, and as you can see I'm living with my cancer. How did things go for you today?' and she smiled a kindly smile.

'Better than I had hoped,' replied Kiri shyly – she wasn't used to speaking to strangers. 'I don't need to come back for three months.'

'I am glad,' said Pauline. Kiri noted Pauline had a way of looking you straight in the eye, without seeming threatening. 'I just wondered if you wanted to come to the support group with me next week. I could do with the company. The friend I usually go with is away visiting her daughter.'

Kiri's first inclination was to say no, but an unusual wave of something brave came over her – she guessed it was that strand of hope again – and she found herself saying yes. The two women arranged to meet outside the community hall at 11 the following Wednesday to go into the meeting together. It was to be the first time Kiri had ever been to a coffee morning in her life and she was rather excited about it.

22

At home a letter was waiting for her on the mat. It was a blue airmail letter from Sri Lanka, which Kiri tore open with delight. Her mother wrote in Sinhalese:

St Mary's School
Coast Road
Batticaloa

My dear sweet Kiribaba,

I was so worried to read your letter. I am doing well, but what about you? I am full of sorrow that your life has been so hard and I didn't even know. You said you had been unwell. What is wrong my darling, and are you alright? Please write again and tell me as much as you can. I pray that you can say you are getting well and strong again. I so want to be with you to help you, but I cannot get myself to England. Can you come to me, dearest girl? It has been too long. Please say you can come to me.

For some time I have been helping out at the girls school here. I work mostly in the kitchen, but sometimes I do cleaning and help care for the smaller girls as well. The school was mostly washed away by the large waters, and it has been awful. We lost some of the children and some teachers to the sea. We don't yet know exactly how many were lost or how many died – I fear it is too many. The school will survive though. We have received some money from a disaster fund, and some from charities and this has enabled us to move into another building nearby. It is little more than a collection of shacks at present, but as I write this the builders are trying to improve it and make it good. They have arranged dormitories for girls who have lost their families, and for staff members who have lost their homes. I have been given a bed here, in a room I share with four other women and I help with the cooking and with anything else I can do. This place has become my home and these people have become my family for now. But you and your brothers in America are my real family. Your brothers have sent some money across the Atlantic and I have put that into the school's funds. I am sorry to tell you that no money has come from Raja yet, but it sounds as if that will be no surprise to you. He sounds a bad husband. Must you stay with him? Let me know if you can come home to me. Write to me again at the school address as soon as you can. Meanwhile know that I love you and always have. The past is in the past.

Your dear mother sends you kisses and prayers.
Mama xx

Kiri wept tears of relief and sadness. Her mama was doing well, but she was so sorry to have added to her worry, when there was so much to worry about in Batticaloa. She had to reply immediately. It felt odd to write in Sinhalese after all these years – she knew her mother spoke quite good English but thought her reading and writing may not be so good:

Dear Mama,

Thank you for your wonderful letter. I am so pleased the school will continue, and that you have found a place for yourself there. You sound so brave and that fills me with pride. Mama, I am going to come back to you. I should not have left as I did, all those years ago. It might take me some time, but when I get to you I will stay. England has not been good for me, but yes, I am getting better. I have suffered from anxiety and depression they say, and I have had breast cancer, but all is good now and I have some tablets to keep me well.

This marriage is over and I plan to leave Raja. I have to sort out the practicalities but I will come soon. Look after those poor children at the school who have lost their homes and their parents. Help them with your love and good cooking. Perhaps when I come I could teach English and read with them – you always said my English was very good.

Until we see each other again, we will both watch the same moon in the sky and think of each other every night. I will write again soon.

With all my love,
Kiribaba xx

Kiri felt warm for the first time in many months. It was now time to share her good news with Penny. Penny answered the phone quickly, as if waiting for the call.

'How are you?' she asked cautiously.

'I'm very good, thank you Penny,' replied Kiri. 'I have my results and I am clear from cancer. They have given me some tablets to stop it returning. Is that the right thing to do? They say they might have side-effects – flushes and dryness, like the menopause. Is that alright?'

'That's fine, Kiri. It sounds like a good idea. Spell the name out for me then I can be sure we are both talking about the same thing. Good, that's fine – as I thought. Now tell me the whole story of your day.'

It was a long call and Penny listened to an animated account of the day from Kiri. It was good to hear this bright woman who less than a month ago had been so cowed and fearful. Penny agreed to pass on the news to Jean, and arranged to drive up to Salford to visit the following weekend. She didn't accept Kiri's offer to stay in the house, but would stay in a bed and breakfast place near Salford Quays which she'd spotted on the internet.

Penny planned to go to see the Lowry Gallery, and do some shopping while she was there and she thought she'd prefer to do that alone. She got more out of art if she was allowed time to absorb it quietly at her own pace. Clive always rushed through a gallery and his comments distracted her. Hettie was too slow and over-analysed things and Theo just seemed to wander round in a daze and they always lost him. Yes, it was better to visit Lowry alone, and that in itself would be a treat and make the long drive from Essex to Manchester doubly worthwhile. She was sure it wouldn't offend Kiri to spend a little time alone.

23

Raja came home in the early evening and remembered to ask Kiri how her clinic appointment had gone. He was pleased she was clear from cancer – he couldn't have faced having to be the supportive husband throughout chemotherapy. At least this way they could keep their distance from each other. He realised that with those meddling women on Kiri's side he would have to give her more freedom, but things need not change too much and perhaps they could lead their own lives under the same roof – lots of couples did that.

When he went upstairs to change his clothes he saw that Kiri had moved all his personal things into the spare room, and made the bed up with fresh sheets. She had made the room tidy and ready for him, and had removed some of the stored clutter so there was even space for an easy chair. He realised this was now his place to be. His brief anger subsided – it might be nice to have some privacy and he still had his treasured study.

'Have you found your new room?' said a voice behind him. 'I thought this would be for the best, at least for the time being. Please do not complain. If you do not like this room you can go to a guest house or rent room at the hospital.'

'This will do for now,' he replied somewhat grudgingly.

'Good. Let us try to be civilised then the police need not be informed. I will still keep house and cook for us both unless I am busy, in which case I will ask you to eat at the hospital, but I would like an agreed housekeeping allowance. I no longer wish to penny pinch and I will not show you receipts for my shopping. Those days are over Raja. I will also need a set of my own house keys for the front and back doors. Oh, and by the way Penny is coming to see me next weekend, so I will be busy and out a lot but don't worry, she will not stay here in the house.'

Kiri turned tail and went back downstairs to make the supper, leaving Raja to his own devices. My goodness, he thought, she's got it all worked out. He wouldn't have imagined her capable of such planning, and it did rather take him by surprise. He sat on the side of the bed and pondered – I'll go with it for now. I'll see how things go. He wasn't sure he had much choice in the short term, and the long term depended on other things, most notably of course, Ria.

So the days of Raja's leave passed by relatively peaceably. Kiri ignored him as much as possible and Raja went out driving a lot. If he was in the house he stayed in his study, apart from meal times, when they sat together and ate in silence. A housekeeping allowance had been agreed and Kiri started to enjoy trips to the market and the grocery store on her own. At each outing she felt braver and her confidence grew as her panic attacks faded into the past. She bought new kinds of food to try out and extended her cooking repertoire. It was a joy to make her own choices without Raja breathing down her neck, criticising and checking prices and receipts. If only she had known how easy it would be to get control back, she could have done it earlier, but perhaps the timing wasn't right before. Now the time was right and fate had come to show her the way.

On Wednesday Kiri dressed carefully in her best tunic and trouser outfit. It was a soft golden brown colour and went well with her green winter coat and tan leather boots. The day was cold and she added a woollen scarf to her outfit before setting off to the community centre to meet Pauline. She found Pauline waiting outside as planned, wearing a pink cloche hat which she kept on throughout the coffee morning, even when the room got hot. There was a brief talk from a bra-fitting lady who had brought samples to show the group of women. She demonstrated special bras for women who'd had mastectomies, and showed them the prosthetic inserts they could choose. Kiri had never seen such beautiful underwear. Since her mastectomy she had managed with the same old bras she'd had before and padded them with handkerchiefs. She was small-breasted so got away with it, but realised now she could be much more comfortable. She didn't have enough money to place an order today, but wrote down the details of the size and style that would suit her, for the next time.

Coffee or tea with biscuits was served for fifty pence – Kiri could manage that from her funds. She sat and talked with her new friends and listened to Pauline, who told more of her story.

Pauline was just 38 years old. She had been married to Andy for five years and just when they were hoping to start a family she found a breast lump. It proved to be an aggressive form of cancer which needed treatment with surgery, chemotherapy and radiotherapy. All was well for four years until she started to get back pain. A scan revealed bony spread – metastatic secondaries they called it. She had more radiotherapy which helped the pain and was now in the middle of some more chemotherapy. This lot was harder and stronger than the last and she had lost all her hair and became anaemic. They gave her blood transfusions to help when her blood count got too low – she'd had one last week, so was feeling a bit better this week. Her chemo was on a three-week cycle, and one week she felt like shit, one week she was just about OK and the third week she felt quite good, just in time to start again. This week was her good week. Kiri listened in awe, amazed at the simple way Pauline told her story, which continued:

Andy had been marvellous throughout and she didn't know what she would do without him. They knew they couldn't have children now, but as long as they had each other that was all that mattered. Andy had a good job with a local furniture manufacturer and his bosses were really good if he needed time off to be with Pauline. Pauline was signed off sick from her job in a department store in the Trafford Centre. She usually worked in the hats and accessory department, and said how handy that was now she needed so many hats and scarves. She even managed to laugh when she said that, and Kiri thought how brave she sounded, especially when she said she'd like to arrange a fashion show when she felt better, showcasing hats, in aid of Breakthrough Breast Cancer.

'Andy and I had planned to go to Sri Lanka for our honeymoon in 2000, to a place called Mount Lavinia. Do you know it – it's just south of Colombo I think?' said Pauline. 'The civil war flared up at the time and we were forced to cancel our plans, and then what with one thing and another we never managed to rearrange it. You know how it is. I'd love you to tell me about your country some time. Would you do that? It sounds such a lovely island.'

Kiri was moved by Pauline's story, and amazed at this woman's resilience. It made her feel guilty – how pathetic she'd been, coping so poorly with her own difficulties which now seemed small in comparison. She felt too ashamed to share her problems with this fine young woman.

'Pauline, you have told me such a sad story. How do you keep smiling through all of this?' she asked. 'I think you are a wonderful example to us all. I would love to tell you all about Sri Lanka, and also I would love to help you with your fashion show. I think it's a splendid idea. How would I be able to help?'

'You can help by being my friend, and I think from the look on your face that you will be a good friend,' Pauline's replied. 'Next week will be my bad week, but we can meet up the week after and talk again. Then you might tell me about your life and about your country. I know things are hard there at the moment but I still want to hear about your life before the troubles.'

'I'd like that very much,' said Kiri. 'It will help me just to think and talk about it too. I miss the place so very much.'

'Let's exchange phone numbers and we can arrange a time and day when I'm up to it. Come to my house for coffee. Andy will be back at work the week after next and I'd like the company.'

Kiri walked home feeling pleased with her morning, but humbled by what she had heard. There were gentle flakes of snow falling on her as she walked and she turned her face upwards to feel the caress of the snow as it melted on her cheeks. The cold English weather usually got her down, but today the snow felt good.

24

Raja went out driving a lot. He went out in his car most days and usually drove past Ria's flat but never caught sight of her. He'd tried to phone her but just got the 'number unobtainable' message – she must have changed her number. One day he rang the doorbell but there was no answer. He tried the door and it was locked, so he poked a little note under the threshold asking her to phone him – he guessed she never would. That's that then, he thought with sadness and a hint of bitterness.

He continued his drives, even as the snow built up. It turned brown and mucky on the roadsides but was oh, so pretty when he left the town and made for the countryside. He often set out to Saddleworth Moor where he would wallow in the loneliness and solitude he found there. He'd park up and gaze out at the derelict landscape and simply think. Self pity led to a dull sadness.

The day after leaving the note for Ria, he set off once more in this now familiar direction. The snow had stopped falling but he could feel the ice under his wheels as he drove eastwards across the moor on the A635. The sun was low in the wintery sky. Raja gave himself a good talking to as he drove his beloved car, telling himself he must get a grip and regain control of his life – even make some new beginnings and shake off this invasive moroseness.

He wasn't concentrating on the road and at a particularly sharp bend he skidded off towards a ditch. He felt himself in suspended animation. The Mercedes caught a wheel on a rock as it descended into the ditch, there was a huge crunching jolt, and the car flipped over. There was a moment of panic, metal on stone, a screech of pain and then nothing.

There wasn't much traffic on the road that day. Some minutes later a white van came along. The driver, a carpenter on his way home to Holmfirth, stopped when he saw the upturned car. He jumped out to investigate and found an unconscious man with his head smashed into the windscreen of the crushed Mercedes. The car's bonnet still felt slightly warm but its occupant was already cold. The carpenter realised he wasn't unconscious, but dead, with his head at a bizarre and totally wrong angle and a frayed seatbelt dangling uselessly across his broken neck – the first aid course at work and his new resuscitation skills were useless. He dialled 999 on his mobile.

The paramedics came quickly and confirmed the carpenter's findings, pronouncing the driver dead at the scene. The police weren't far behind and began their investigations. He'd have died immediately they told the carpenter when they took his statement.

An hour or two later Kiri heard a knock at her door. She opened it to find a policeman and policewoman standing on her doorstep in the cold, fading light.

Kiri felt numb when they told her that her husband had been involved in an accident on Saddleworth Moor and had been declared dead at the scene. She shuddered when she remembered her thoughts about severed brake lines.

'How? Why? What was he doing on Saddleworth Moor?' she stammered when she found her voice. Her heart had lost its normal rhythm and she felt as if she was floating above her own body.

The WPC made her the obligatory cup of tea and they sat awhile as the news sank in.

'Can we call anyone for you?' asked the policewoman who'd introduced herself as 'WPC Jones, but call me Linda.'

'Pardon? No, I mean I don't know,' replied Kiri. She turned her good ear to the woman – in times of stress her poor hearing always deteriorated and she found it hard to hear Linda's calming, reassuring voice. 'I wouldn't know who to call,' she added.

'How about family, or friends, or a neighbour?' suggested Linda.

'There is no-one,' replied Kiri quietly, 'but my friend from Essex is coming to see me at the weekend. I'll be alright till then. I'm quite used to being on my own here.'

'This situation is rather different Mrs Coomaraswamy, and we would advise you to have someone with you. There are practical things you might want help with too. We would like you to come to the hospital in Manchester to identify the body as soon as you feel able, and you should have someone with you for that at least. What do you think?' Linda was starting to feel concerned for this poor woman.

Kiri couldn't phone Pauline – it was her bad week, and Penny was too far away and would be at work until the weekend. She wondered what sort of thing Shelley meant about asking if she needed help. She wondered if the policewoman could somehow see her guilty thoughts.

'I do have a friend at the hospital in Manchester – well she's a social worker actually, but also a friend. I think I might phone her.'

'Great,' said Linda who passed Kiri her mobile phone with Shelley's number stored on the contact list. Thank goodness Shelley picked up.

'Hello, is that you Shelley? It's Kiri de Souza here.'

The police officers raised their eyebrows at the different name.

'I have had some bad news, Shelley, and I think I need some help and advice. I'm passing the phone now to a nice policewoman who is here with me. Her name is Linda.'

Linda explained the situation as discreetly as possible and Shelley nobly offered to meet them later at the Chapel of Rest at the Royal Infirmary. Shelley then spoke to Kiri.

'Kiri, this is terrible. Of course I'll help in whatever way I can. I'm still in the office at work but I can get over to the Royal Infirmary easily, so I'll meet you there if you go with the police. They'll look after you. Kiri, you know if you don't feel up to identifying the body we could ask someone else? We could contact Raja's boss, Mr Thompson. He might do it to save you the trauma. It might not be a pretty sight you know?' said Shelley.

'I think I need to do it myself or I might not believe it's true,' said Kiri. 'They say there has to be an autopsy and an inquest. I won't know what to do next. I don't know how to arrange a funeral, and who will tell his parents? Oh dear, oh dear! I don't know what to do, Shelley.'

Then the tears came – silently, big plopping tears fell down her cheeks and splashed on to her lap. She had no control over them and couldn't tell if they were tears of sorrow, shock, guilt, grief or relief.

After a while the tears dried up. Linda passed a box of tissues and when the time seemed right she gently asked, 'Kiri, do you feel up to a journey to Manchester tonight? I guess it would wait till tomorrow.'

'I shall be fine. I'll just go and wash my face, then let's get it over with. There will be so much to do, so why delay?'

'You are very brave,' said the WPC.

'Pardon? Sorry, I have trouble with my hearing.'

'I said you are very brave,' she repeated.

'No I'm not,' said Kiri, 'but what choice do I have? This isn't bravery, this is inevitability.'

The journey to central Manchester was quick and soon they were outside the hospital's bereavement suite where Shelley was waiting. The two police officers said they would be in touch again once they had spoken to the Coroner's Officer. Linda gave Kiri her contact details on a card and they left her in Shelley's capable hands. Kiri wondered what Linda's policeman accomplice actually did. Very little it seemed – she did all the talking and he just seemed to sit there. Still he was a good driver. She'd always thought Raja was a good driver. Shows how wrong you can be, she thought.

The bereavement officer introduced himself as Malcolm. All these 'officers' thought Kiri – coroner's officers, bereavement officers, I wonder who next? She realised her mind was wandering and had to make herself concentrate on what the kindly man was saying. Malcolm was an older man, grey-haired and very camp indeed. He told them he was a retired nurse who had retrained to do this job. He directed his soft gaze at Kiri and explained the procedure of identifying the body to her, giving her plenty of time to change her mind if she so wished.

Kiri went ahead and performed the dreadful task – she was pleased with herself for going through with it. That man who had made her life so miserable was indeed dead, and in death he looked more like the handsome chap she had known in Sri Lanka. The mortuary officials had arranged a clever sheet around his neck and one side of his head, shielding her from the worst of it and what she saw was a composed, relaxed face which was remarkably unmarked. She didn't want details of his fatal injuries just yet, but reality was sinking in and she started to shake uncontrollably.

Back in his office with Shelley and a cup of sweet tea, Malcolm went on to explain the need for an autopsy – the case would be referred to the Coroner's Officer, a special police officer who worked with the Coroner. The Coroner would be the one to issue the death certificate, which had to be done before the body could be released for burial or cremation. Malcolm gave Kiri a booklet with all the details she would need about the next steps, and told her simply to wait for the Coroner's Officer to make contact with her in the morning. He suggested she might like to think about which undertaker to use. Kiri looked blank.

'Her husband was Hindu,' chipped in Shelley. 'Could you advise us of the options?'

'In this area we have several who are familiar with the needs of the Hindu community, but these are the firms I would suggest.' Malcolm passed a short list to Shelley for safe keeping.

The two women stepped out into the cold night air feeling relieved to escape the oppressive atmosphere of Malcolm's office. However kind he was it was a grizzly subject to have to talk about, and this was just the beginning. Shelley drove Kiri home planning to stay a while but not all night – she had her pets to feed and look after at home. She lived alone and had an early morning meeting the next day on the other side of the city, so couldn't be too late.

'That's no problem. I am used to being alone in this house. Even when Raja was here I felt alone. I did love him once you know, a long time ago, but I don't believe he ever really loved me,' said Kiri, as much to herself as to her friend.

Shelley phoned Penny to impart the news, then went to the kitchen to make beans on toast for their tea while Kiri took over the phone call. Penny was aghast. This was unbelievable – thank goodness Shelley was there with Kiri.

'I'll come down as planned on Friday afternoon, and yes, I'll drive extra carefully,' she promised.

As they ate their beans on toast – well, Shelley ate and

Kiri just picked at hers – the two women talked. Shelley was intrigued to hear more about the traditions of the Hindu faith. She knew they believed in reincarnation and disapproved of divorce but she knew little if anything about their funeral traditions. Kiri knew that they liked to bury or cremate a body within twenty-hour hours of death if possible, but that would be impossible with an autopsy to delay things. Apparently a priest or brahman would chant a mantra at the funeral and offerings of rice and milk might be made. Married people were usually cremated, not buried, and their ashes were strewn in one of the holy rivers of India.

'Oh my gosh – someone must tell Raja's parents, I can't do it. I've never actually met them. They wouldn't talk to me after we were married – they think I am the devil and that everything that went wrong was my fault. How can I tell them their eldest son is no more? What if they want his ashes returned to India? How can I arrange that?'

Tears of helplessness and confusion sprang once more to her eyes. She knew these tears were for herself and not Raja, and that made her feel even worse. She didn't know how she was meant to feel at a time like this.

'Don't worry about that for tonight,' said Shelley. 'We can work something out when the time comes. I think you should ask the Coroner's Officer to inform Raja's family in India. He is a police officer who is skilled in that sort of thing. I'm sure he'll advise you if you ask him in the morning and we'll ask the undertaker about the ashes. OK?'

They were both getting tired but Shelley realised Kiri wouldn't even try to rest until her mind was more settled. The last job of the day was to write a list of people who had to be informed of the death – Mr Thompson and the administrators at the Royal Hospital, the bank, the GP if Raja actually had one, their solicitor, utility companies and the internet provider. There probably would be more but that would do for a start, thought Shelley. They must have a solicitor to have bought their house, but Kiri didn't know who it was. As for a will perhaps the bank or the solicitor might know if there was one.

'I really must be getting home now, Kiri. Most of this will wait until you get the death certificate from the Coroner. You won't be able to do much without a certificate anyway. Tell you what, shall I make the call to Mr Thompson in the morning, just to get started on that list?' asked Shelley.

'Yes, thank you so much. That will get us started. Now go home and see to your pets. I've kept you too long already,' replied Kiri. She suddenly needed to be alone.

'It's not been a problem. I'm so glad you phoned me.' Shelley patted Kiri's hand. 'I'll pop in after work tomorrow and see how things are going, but phone me if you need me. Now do try to get a little rest.'

Kiri clasped Shelley's hand briefly, and then let her go. She locked the door behind her and was then was truly alone in the house which she presumed was now her own.

25

Kiri didn't sleep until the early hours of the morning. She lay on top of her bed feeling once again like her old, useless and anxious self. She didn't love Raja, but he had made her dependent on him, and he had become part of her even though he hurt her. He'd controlled her life for so many years and she wondered how she would cope alone. She had only just begun to learn not to fear him – and not to fear life itself – and she could still barely stand on her own two feet. She hoped her new friends would be enough for her, at least until she got back to Sri Lanka – if only she had never left.

She fretted over the effect Raja's death would have on his elderly parents and his brother but she doubted many other people would be affected by his loss. How sad that there were not hordes of his friends to consider and contact with the news. His life was almost as depleted as hers, and despite his bullying and external confidence he was no happier than she was. As she drifted into a fitful sleep she admitted that in the end she had not been a good wife for him – perhaps it was all her fault, as he'd always told her.

She woke up feeling horrible, clammy and dirty. She ran herself a warm bath and soaked in the soapy water, trying to cleanse herself of the wretched thoughts of the night. She dressed but couldn't face breakfast. She could only manage endless cups of tea and she sat at the kitchen table in a befuddled state. The doorbell brought her back to the present. Two police officers were at the door – a different male officer, more senior it seemed, and WPC Linda Jones from last night. It was the senior man who did the talking this time, and he used a very different tone. There had been a development overnight and they wanted her to accompany them to the station to give a statement.

'I don't understand. I have nothing to tell you. I was here at home as you know,' she said looking pleadingly Linda. 'Am I being arrested? What for? Can I phone my friend?'

'All will be explained at the station and we can phone your friend from there,' replied the senior officer. 'Can I advise you to simply come with us for now.'

When Kiri got to the interview room at the police station they kept asking her questions about the frayed seatbelt. They went on and on about the seatbelt, even though Kiri told them it had been frayed for months. They questioned her about her relationship with Raja and she had to admit it wasn't good, but managed to avoid telling them about his abuse and violence towards her. He'd instilled such secrecy in her over the years it was still second nature to keep quiet about such personal things. Kiri got more and more agitated and upset at the persistent questioning, and only when Shelley arrived with a duty solicitor was the problem revealed.

The police had found a sharp kitchen knife down the side of the car's back seat and they were suspicious that Kiri had tampered with the seatbelt. Kiri explained away the knife's presence clearly and repeatedly. They took her fingerprints and put her in a locked room to wait for she knew not what. Ages later and after a long private debate with the solicitor, they returned. They let her go home, but told her not to go anywhere. The forensic results from the knife and the seatbelt would be available tomorrow.

Kiri was in such a state of exhaustion and anxious confusion that Shelley thought it unsafe to leave her. Kiri just kept mumbling under her breath, 'I have done nothing, I have done nothing, I have done nothing,' and Shelley could do nothing to calm her. The two women had a sleepless night, waiting.

The police were at her door again at 10 o'clock. Kiri held her breath as they spoke to her. She'd explained over and over that the kitchen knife was taken on their trip to peel fruit. They'd taken apples for a snack, but hadn't eaten them and she'd then forgotten all about the knife. The knife must have slipped from her pocket and lodged between the seats. She never mentioned it was also to be her weapon if Raja attacked her – that seemed irrelevant now. She never mentioned the thoughts about brake lines, or slashed wrists. She just kept thinking, stupid, stupid knife.

The senior police man spoke with aggressive authority, 'Mrs Coomaraswamy, we have the results back from our laboratories and we can confirm that the fibres on the seatbelt show no sign of recent cutting with a knife. The fraying had been caused by blunt trauma and appears to have taken place a long time ago. There are no seatbelt fibres on the knife, which does of course bear your fingerprints. All this evidence confirms your story and we are therefore taking this no further. This information will all be presented to the Coroner at the inquest, but I don't think we need to trouble you any further. You may still be called to give evidence.'

Kiri didn't know whether to be relieved or cross at the policeman's manner. Thankfully Shelley stepped in,

'Well, thank you for that. It's just a shame you had to upset my friend at this difficult time, but we understand you were only doing your job. Can you now leave us in peace to grieve and make our arrangements? Will all this delay the death certificate?'

The policeman replied that it should now be straightforward and the Coroner's Officer would be in touch. He marched away with the silent WPC following obediently, with eyes down.

'I think Linda Jones was a little embarrassed by that,' Shelley remarked.

Shelley and Kiri sat on the sofa taking stock. Already news of the accident was starting to spread – there was a report of the accident in the papers, with a picture of the smashed-up Mercedes in the local gazette, and an item about it on the local radio news. Kiri knew the news would not have spread to Bangalore yet and that still worried her – they had to be told. She had never spoken to her in-laws and wasn't sure if she was up to this as their first conversation. They would be very old – they might even be dead by now, and if not the shock might kill them. She didn't even know their address. She told Shelley she'd come across a Canadian phone number for Raja's brother, Rupesh, the dentist and favourite son, and she might be able to phone him later, but there was no rush. She was stalling and needed time to think about what to say. She needed to work out the time difference in Canada before she could do this awful job – anything to delay it.

Shelley had already informed Mr Thompson, who was visibly shaken by the news. He wasn't exactly close to Raja, nor were they fond of each other, but they had known each other for many years, and Mr Thompson had regarded Raja as a diligent and reliable colleague. When Mr Thompson announced the death to the rest of the department it was the registrar, Jack, who most shared his shock.

Just a couple of nights ago Jack had tracked down the nurse, Ria, through their mutual friend, Helena. Helena and Ria had arranged to meet for a drink at the Rose and Crown and Helena said that some other people from the hospital might come along. Ria had not been out since her fall and was pleased to have a change of scene. She agreed to go just as long as Raja wasn't going to be there. When Ria arrived at the pub Jack and

Helena were deep in conversation but stopped abruptly as she approached them. Ria got the feeling they were talking about her and wondered if there was a hidden agenda to this meeting. Ria and Jack were formally introduced and both thought they recognised each other from the hospital corridors and were amazed they had not met before.

The conversation was light-hearted and sociable, and Jack and Ria seemed to get on surprisingly well. She liked the way his look penetrated her being – all-knowing, so sure of himself. He didn't exactly flirt but she could feel a frisson of attraction stirring between them. When he made his excuses to leave he asked if they might meet again and they exchanged phone numbers. Jack was almost ten years younger than Ria and she had to admit to feeling flattered by his attention – pleased she hadn't lost her touch. Helena raised her eyebrows and the women laughed together for a while before Helena broke the mood and quizzed Ria about the fall. Ria swore her to secrecy when she admitted the full extent of her relationship with Raja. Helena knew already but said nothing. Ria played down the role of Mr Morris as much as possible – there was only so much confessing one could do in one evening. Even though Ria remained vague about the fall, Helena was sure she could read between the lines – she'd seen it all before in Casualty. She urged Ria to come clean and speak to the police.

'No,' said Ria. 'It's over. That man is out of my life, and that is all that matters. I am moving departments and making a new start. He might have done me a favour actually.' She gave her friend a mischievous smile and a wink. 'Dinner with Jack might turn out to be fun. I haven't had a toy-boy for ages.'

Helena gasped. 'Ria, you are incorrigible.'

So that morning after hearing Mr Thompson's bombshell Jack's first thought was of Ria. He wondered if she knew. He didn't know her well enough to drop that one on her himself so he decided to phone Helena, and Helena slipped across to the flat during her lunch break. She saw the morning edition of the local gazette on Ria's coffee table and the two women's eyes met. They hugged each other and no words were spoken. Ria was feeling sick even before Helena's visit. When Helena left her she rushed to the bathroom and vomited.

* * *

The Coroner's Officer phoned Kiri at the end of the week. He offered to come to her house with an interim death certificate and the several copies she would need. Kiri made him tea and he went through the details with her. The cause of death was recorded as a broken neck and he said a faulty seatbelt was involved.

'He did complain the seatbelt was frayed and awkward,' she said. 'I told the police all about it. I told him to get it fixed.'

'I know. There'll be an inquest at a later stage. We will inform you when and you might be asked to give more information at the time,' said the officer, 'but for now we can release the body to the undertakers and you can make your arrangements. I cannot stay with you, I'm afraid. I am on my way to a meeting. I'm very sorry. Can I phone someone for you?'

Why do they all ask that, thought Kiri? It must be in their training manual that people cannot be left alone. 'I am content to be alone,' she answered, 'I have a friend coming later.'

Alone once more, Kiri went into Raja's study and worked her way through more of his papers, putting together facts about his life – a life she had known so little about. Shelley had helped her to start the process and she added names and addresses to the contact list they had made. Shelley had promised to get the phone changed to enable outgoing calls and was also keen to change the internet account to Kiri's name before it got closed down. She'd promised to give Kiri computer lessons when they had time, but needed a password to access the machine before she could do anything.

'Think of a password he might have used,' she had asked Kiri. 'Go on, suggest some words or names for me.'

Kiri looked at Shelley blankly at first, then responded, 'Try Kiribaba. No? OK, Mercedes, or Bangalore, or Kandy? I know – try Charmina.'

'Yes, that's it. We're in,' said Shelley. 'Who the heck's Charmina?'

'She's the woman my husband should have married,' Kiri had replied with a flat voice, devoid of emotion.

This morning the computer was still no use to her, even if she now knew the password. Kiri had no idea how to use it yet, but one day she would learn, she thought, as she ran her fingers over the keys.

She sat at Raja's desk with the death certificate and several copies of it under her hand. Time to get on with things, she decided – she dialled the undertaker's office on her mobile to confirm a provisional appointment arranged by Shelley. She wondered whether to phone Canada but thought it was too early and would be too difficult on a mobile. She might just wait until the phone line was fixed.

She poked about in more of Raja's secret drawers, throwing away rubbish but keeping documents that looked important. She made up her own filing system and was pleased with the order she created. In the bottom drawer she found adverts for an escort company and some business cards with phone numbers for 'Special Massage' and 'Personal Treatments', and other such delights. She felt grubby just looking at them. She plugged in the shredder and destroyed them, along with a pile of gambling chits.

In another drawer was a small picture of a petite dark-haired woman. She had a Mediterranean look about her and a broad smile which lit up an otherwise plain face. Kiri didn't recognise the woman but decided to keep the picture along with two others – a sepia print of Raja's parents on their wedding day, and a picture of a beautiful Asian woman. I know who that one is, thought Kiri. She felt sad when she realised there was no picture of her anywhere in his room, not even from their happier early days.

The last job she gave herself that day before Penny arrived was to phone Pauline. She waited till late afternoon in case Pauline was resting, and hoping Andy would be home with her. Andy answered:

'I'm sorry, Kiri, but she's not here at the moment. She was readmitted to hospital last night with blood poisoning after last week's chemo knocked out her white blood cells. She's in Lewis Ward at the Christie. I've just got back from visiting. She's got a drip up and is improving already, so they say she'll be home in a few days. Shall I give her a message?'

'No, just send her my love and tell her I'll be in touch,' replied Kiri.

That sounded bad – poor Pauline. I can't face phoning Canada now – it'll wait till tomorrow, she thought, as she pressed the little red phone on her mobile to end the call.

26

Penny checked into a carefully chosen boutique hotel and unpacked before making her way to Autumn Avenue. The women greeted each other with consoling hugs. Kiri didn't let go for ages and Penny simply waited until she felt the strength return to her trembling friend.

'It's so good to see you,' said the little Sri Lankan woman, who stood almost a head shorter than Penny. They were such opposites in type and style, and seemed unlikely friends. Penny was tall and robust with an athletic build. She had wavy brown hair, tinted with subtle golden highlights, and wore discreet but flattering make-up which made her look younger than her years. She was elegant yet casual in her designer jeans and cashmere jumper, topped with a padded Barbour jacket. She slipped off her fleece-lined leather boots on the mat before entering the living room.

Kiri had spruced herself up a little for the visit, but never wore make-up. The cares of life had worn away her youthful face but her complexion was still clear, apart from a few lines at the corners of her eyes. How unkind to say 'crow's feet' thought Penny, but she couldn't think of a better term to use – 'laughter lines' was an even less appropriate word in someone who had laughed so little in recent years. Kiri's long dark hair was still glossy but a shadow of ghostly greyness was appearing at the temples. Today she wore casual brown trousers and a beige tunic-style jumper which grazed her slim hips. An intricate pendant embellished the neckline. She looked thin and shrunken compared with the bonny girl Penny used to know. Penny hoped all this was reversible and that once returned to full health, both physically and emotionally, Kiri would once again thrive.

Over tea they talked and caught up with events. Kiri told Penny the story as she knew it, and Penny came to appreciate the severity of Kiri's plight. This isolated woman had so much to deal with and for the most part would have to deal with things alone, in a country where even after twenty years she still felt alien. The practical demands of Raja's death were overwhelming, and for now were masking most of Kiri's emotions, but Penny knew in due course there would be a complex grieving process to get through – guilt, anger, sadness and relief, then no doubt more guilt.

'It's good to have you to talk to, Penny, and also I have some jobs I need help with. Do you mind if I ask?' said Kiri.

'Ask away – whatever you want. That's what I'm here for, I want to help,' replied Penny.

'I have an appointment with the undertaker tomorrow morning and I wondered if you would come with me?'

'No problem. Of course I'll come. Mind you, I don't know much about Hindu funerals,' said Penny. 'What else is on your list?'

'Well, I haven't managed to inform Raja's family yet. I meant to ask the Coroner's Officer to help but I forgot. It is just too difficult for me to speak to Raja's parents myself. I have never spoken to them but I know they hate me. They think I ruined their little king's life. Did you know the name Raja means King? Anyway I don't have a phone number for the old couple, but I have found a number for Raja's brother, Rupesh, in Canada and I thought I might phone him while you are here, so you can help me if I falter.'

'Oh, Kiri, they must be told. Yes perhaps it'll be easier to go through Rupesh. I like that name – it's rather unusual. Let's phone him now. It must be early afternoon in Canada. I'll get through to him, and then I could hand over to you. OK? But first tell me a bit about him so I know what to expect.'

Kiri filled in some background.

'I was told the name Rupesh means Lord of Beauty. Raja called him Ru if he ever spoke of him, which wasn't often. I met him once when he visited England in the early days of our marriage. Raja was always jealous of his younger brother, who was much taller and more handsome than he was. Apparently both boys were bright at school, but Rupesh was the charming, sociable one, and Rupesh was their parents' favourite.'

'Oh, that must have been tough on Raja,' commented Penny.

'Yes,' agreed Kiri, 'but Ru struggled with it too. He found it very oppressive and escaped as soon as he could. He went to be a dentist in Canada and never returned. He married a Canadian girl called Mandy, and they had two beautiful children, and a seemingly perfect life. Raja found all that intolerable and broke off all contact with his brother seven or eight years ago as far as I know.'

'Coo, a psychologist would have a field day with all that,' remarked Penny. 'Right, let's get on with this call – you or me?'

'You start it off and I'll take over if it's going alright,' said Kiri.

'Good plan,' agreed Penny.

Penny jotted down a few notes to refer to, and dialled the long international number. The phone was answered by a strong female voice with a Canadian accent. The voice sounded cautious when Penny asked to speak to Rupesh Coomaraswamy.

'May I ask who is calling? This is his wife speaking – Mandy Coomaraswamy.'

'You don't know me but I am calling about Rupesh's brother, Raja, and it is rather important. Is he there?'

'OK. I'll see if I can find him.'

'Ru Coomaraswamy speaking. Can I help you?'

Penny introduced herself as a friend of Raja and Kiri, then using her professional voice she calmly informed Rupesh of his brother's fatal accident. The man was silent for a moment, then Penny heard him muffle the receiver and mumble to his wife who was obviously still there. His voice came back to her, asking questions as he tried to compute what had happened. He wanted to speak to Kiri now. He sounded a reasonable man and they would have to communicate some time, she thought.

'Hello, Kiri – Mandy and I send you our condolences. It is quite a shock. I don't know what to say. How are you?' he asked.

'Thank you for asking. I am managing,' replied Kiri politely. 'The thing is, Rupesh, no-one has yet informed your parents. Could you do it? I have never actually spoken to them.'

'Wow, really, never? Well I guess it might come best from me then. They are pretty old and frail now and rather forgetful, I'm afraid. They are looked after by a housekeeper these days. They would never manage a journey to England for the funeral. But yes, I'll speak to them. I might have to go to them – I'm thinking out loud now, sorry. I'll get back to you about that idea, so leave it with me. Now, what are you doing about a funeral?'

Kiri told him that she and Penny would go to the funeral directors in the morning to discuss the options, but that it would be a cremation. It would be a help if Rupesh could think about the ashes and they would speak again the next evening.

'Just one more thing – I think you should know we did not have a happy marriage. There were many problems, but even so I will try to do right by him,' said Kiri before she hung up.

Ru put the phone down and fell into his wife's waiting arms, where he quietly wept for his poor lost, jealous, unhappy brother.

27

Penny drove Kiri to the Co-op funeral parlour, where the discreet office was filled with a pervading air of reverence. The undertaker, Mr Black, was a bowed-over Mancunian with a slightly obsequious manner. Despite his Dickensian appearance they warmed to him as he spoke competently and professionally, apparently very knowledgeable, even about the Hindu traditions. He told them Manchester had a significant Hindu community and his firm had good connections with the Shree Krishna Manir Temple and their pujari.

'What's a pujari?' asked Penny, who was fascinated by these cultural revelations.

'He's their spiritual leader I believe, and the temple is run by trustees and volunteers who work with him. The good news is they are happy to compromise and help with funerals, even if the deceased was not a member of their temple. I gather you are not a Hindu, Mrs Coomaraswamy.'

'I am not,' said Kiri, 'and after we came to England my husband did not attend temple, or worship as far as I am aware. I do think however that we should honour his background and bring Hindu traditions into the service. I was wondering if we could ask a brahman, or do I mean pujari, to conduct a ceremony at the local crematorium rather than at the temple? Do you think that would that be possible? I don't think there will be a big gathering of mourners and I'd prefer to keep it simple.'

Mr Black seemed to think this would work and promised to speak to the trustees at the temple and start to make arrangements. These days they were getting used to mixed faith services in this mixed-up world.

Kiri and Penny left him to it and went for a light lunch at a nearby cafe. They ate sandwiches followed by ice-cream with chocolate sauce, to recharge their batteries, and Kiri made her next request to Penny.

'I need something to wear at the cremation. They wear white as the colour of mourning and I have nothing suitable. I would like to buy a white tunic or blouse and a white three-quarter length coat which I could wear over a long black skirt. Do you think that would do?'

'Sounds good to me – let's go shopping. We can go to the Trafford Centre. I gather it's huge, with a vast choice of shops.'

Kiri remembered Pauline saying she worked there in a big department store.

'Trafford Centre here we come then,' said Penny, who, even though she said so herself, was an expert shopper.

Kiri was overcome by the size and bustle of the shopping centre. It made her feel hot and sweaty, and very uncomfortable, so they made straight for Pauline's store and Kiri sat while Penny brought her items to look at.

'Is this what they mean by a personal shopper?' joked Kiri, as she started to feel more settled.

They chose an outfit for Kiri, and a silk top in a rich burgundy colour for Penny, who just couldn't resist a purchase for herself. On the way back to the car Kiri had an idea – 'Have we time to call in at the hospital for ten minutes to see how Pauline is? I don't think it's too far.'

'Good thought. You haven't told her about Raja yet have you? If she's well enough it might be better face to face than over the phone,' said Penny.

They easily found Lewis Ward with just half an hour of visiting time to go. Andy was sitting at Pauline's bedside, and Pauline was sitting up looking pretty and pink, with a crushed raspberry-coloured turban arrangement on her head – quite perky having just had a pint of blood dripped into her veins. She was going to be allowed home the next day, she said. Andy tactfully slipped out for a cup of coffee in the canteen and left the women to talk. Pauline was sad to hear Kiri's news. She didn't know Raja personally but felt huge sympathy for her new friend.

'Next week will be my good week,' she said. 'Come round to my house for coffee on Monday morning at ten and we'll talk some more.'

They didn't stay long and on the way home Penny commented on what a brave and lovely woman Pauline seemed to be, and just the sort of friend Kiri needed. She imagined that Kiri might make a good friend for Pauline and Andy too, if the going got tough for them. Kiri might like having someone to care for – it would take her out of herself and make her feel useful again. Kiri recounted how the couple had missed their honeymoon in Sri Lanka, and that they had planned to stay at the Mount Lavinia Hotel.

'Gosh, I remember Mount Lavinia,' recalled Penny. 'Jean and I used to go there to swim and sunbathe if we wanted to get out of Colombo. We'd take the bus and go to the posh hotel pretending to be rich tourists rather than poor students. We used to order fresh lime juice and sit on the terrace in the sun, waited on by the charming waiters who made a great fuss of two English girls out on their own. Most of the tourists in those days were Germans who took private cars or taxis everywhere, so we caused quite a stir on the buses too. The only Europeans on public transport tended to be travellers on the hippy trail and we didn't quite fit that description.'

'I love to hear you talk about Sri Lanka and the fact that you loved my country so much,' said Kiri. 'I do wonder if it will ever be the same there after the war and the tsunami, but we are resilient people.'

'We certainly had a wonderful time there. I've brought my old photograph album to show you if we have time later, and I do believe there are some pictures of Mount Lavinia in it. You must take it to show Pauline next week,' offered Penny.

'Could I really? That would be wonderful. But don't you want to take the album home with you?'

'No, you can keep it for a while. Clive has scanned all the best pictures on to the computer, and enhanced the colours a bit. They were just snaps I took with my little Kodak camera and they've faded rather badly, but they're still worth looking at, and you can return them next time I come.'

'Next time you come could you bring me a copy of that photo of you, me and Jean at the Elephant Orphanage? We all looked so young and happy then. Do you remember the elephant keeper wanted us to pay him five rupees, just for him to take a photo of us with our own camera?' said Kiri.

'Yes, I love that one too,' said Penny. 'I'm sure Clive will do you a copy.'

It pleased Kiri that there was going to be a next time, and that Penny was planning to keep in closer contact from now on. She knew though that Penny had to get back to Essex and her own family tomorrow, then no doubt work on Monday at her GP surgery.

Penny continued, 'When the funeral is over do you think you might like to come and stay with me and Clive for a little holiday?'

'I've never really had a holiday,' admitted Kiri. 'It might be nice, but how would I get there? I don't travel well. I don't think I could manage the train on my own. Perhaps it's too much, but thanks for the thought.'

'You are going to have to travel soon, that is if you really want to get back to Sri Lanka – just take one step at a time. I can come and get you by car the first time and Clive can drive you back. Anyway we'll sort out some sort of plan when the time comes. Let's look at these photos now and get a take-away for supper. Shall we have Indian, Chinese or pizza?'

'Ooh, I'd like to try Chinese but I wouldn't know what to choose,' said Kiri feeling adventurous and useless at the same time.

'It's easy,' said Penny, 'and you just guess if you don't know what something is. It's time you spread your wings, Kiri, and learned to fly.'

Kiri smiled in agreement. If only she was as confident as Penny, life would be so much easier.

'Is Hettie like you?' she asked. 'I mean is she strong and confident and lively?'

'She looks like her father, but has more of my personality I guess, whereas Theo looks like me but is quieter and more thoughtful, like his dad. Actually they are a wonderful mixture of the two of us.'

'You are so lucky. Will they become doctors?' asked Kiri.

'No way – I think we've put them off. Hettie has a plan to study architecture in Brighton or Leeds and Theo hasn't decided yet, but he's very good at history and art. He'll do something arty I think, but there's plenty of time for him to make up his mind.'

'Will you show me some pictures of Hettie and Theo? Might they be at home if I visit you?' Kiri was warming to the idea of a trip to Essex.

Penny was planning a quick scoot round the Lowry exhibition centre before she set off home to Essex the next day, so she said good night after supper and left Kiri to clear the table. Kiri was tired but more content than she'd been for ages as she tidied away the remains of the Chinese meal – Penny said she always over-ordered, and my goodness, she was right. With the table cleared Kiri sat down and wrote a letter. She wrote it in Sinhalese again, and still it felt strange after all these years speaking English.

> Dear Mama,
>
> I have some difficult news to tell you. I have to tell you that my husband Raja is dead. He was killed in a car crash. Thankfully no-one else was hurt. As I write this I can hardly believe it is true, but I know it is because I have seen the body, and now I am having to arrange a funeral. I don't know after all that has happened whether to feel sad or happy, lost or found.
>
> The good news is that my breast cancer has not come back and I am on tablets now to stop it returning. I have made new friends and I am learning to live again.
>
> I truly believe that I will be home with you within the year, and until then, dearest Mama, we must be patient and look after ourselves. Please do not work too hard at the school, however much you love the girls there. I do not want you to wear yourself away before I get there. I know you are not yet 70, but most people in England think of retiring at 65!
>
> Don't worry about your newly widowed daughter. I feel sure I am going to be alright and adapt to my new circumstances. I am feeling stronger each day.
>
> All my love, as always
>
> Kiribaba xx

Kiri looked up at the moon and said, 'I'll post that tomorrow, Mama. Good night.'

28

She slept late on Monday morning and woke up with the thud of post on the door mat. Kiri had never had so much post in her life – there were sympathy cards from Jean, Shelley and Ramona, Mr Thompson and Angie. In his card Mr Thompson had written a lovely note saying how much the department would miss Raja, and that Kiri must let him know if he could do anything to help her. There was an official-looking letter from Mr Black agreeing to arrange the funeral for her, along with a corporate-looking sympathy card from the Co-op funeral service.

Beneath the little pile of cards was a brown envelope. It was a bill for the house contents insurance, asking for an annual payment by cheque. Kiri panicked as she realised she had no access to cheques and did not know how to pay this bill. As far as she knew Raja paid bills by direct debit, but apparently not this one. She wasn't absolutely certain their bank account was even in joint names, but she did remember once signing something for the mortgage, so was reasonably confident the house was in both names. She had an idea the mortgage was paid off by some policy or other if one of them died. She wished now she'd taken more notice of such matters, but then again Raja wouldn't have allowed her to. Now she was left with an incomprehensible muddle of financial chaos.

Kiri made a cup of tea to calm herself before calling Shelley, who had just arrived at work.

'I'm really sorry to bother you so early,' said Kiri breathlessly, 'but can you help me to see the bank manager and the solicitor soon? I don't know what to do about money, and paying bills and things like that. I've spent a lot of my rainy day money already and now I don't know what to do, Shelley. I am so useless.'

'Stop saying that, Kiri. You are not useless. You're doing alright – it's early days yet, so try to stay calm. Why don't you go back to the study and keep working through that paperwork? Put aside anything to do with the house, as well as any financial details or account numbers. I'll be able to call in at lunchtime but I must dash off to a meeting now. Monday mornings can be hectic around here. Alright? Good, see you just after one.'

The morning slipped by, only interrupted by a call from Mr Black to say he'd booked the crematorium and the priest from the temple for Thursday at 11 o'clock. Could she get in to see him tomorrow to run through the fine details and sign some papers for him? Kiri felt brave enough to do this on her own and booked a taxi for a 10 o'clock meeting with him at his office.

In the midst of the muddle of paperwork she found details of a bank account in joint names, which didn't seem to contain much money. To her surprise she found another account, held in his name only and this one shocked her with its contents. So, she thought to herself, not only was he frittering money away on gambling and women, he was also hiding large sums of money away from me. She wondered for what purpose – she might never know – but she realised she may have more money now than she had ever dreamed of, depending on the will of course. Panic set in again because no will had been found and indeed a will might not even exist. She really needed those appointments with the bank and the solicitor as soon as possible.

'You've done well,' said Shelley as she ate a lunchtime sandwich with Kiri. 'I told you that you weren't useless. I'll see if we can get some appointments tomorrow afternoon, when I can be free to meet you after you've seen Mr Black. Do you think you can handle him on your own, because I won't be free till midday?'

'Yes, I've already arranged a taxi to go on my own,' said Kiri proudly.

'Great. You know it might take some time to sort out the cash flow situation. It'll be no trouble to get you a cheque book for the joint account, but as you know everything else depends on the will, and even if these guys know where the will is, Raja's estate will not be sorted out until after the inquest. Did the Coroner's Officer say when that might be?' asked Shelley.

'In about a month I think,' replied Kiri.

'That's not bad. It still takes ages to wind up an estate though.'

'What's this about an estate? He didn't own an estate, just this one house and one Mercedes saloon car.'

Shelley giggled. 'The estate is what the deceased's combined assets or possessions add up to. Oh dear, Kiri, you do need my help after all,' she teased her friend, nudging her playfully in the ribs.

Even Kiri managed a little giggle. 'Well you learn something every day.'

'OK. So I'll collect you from the Co-op at midday. We can go to the solicitor first then have a quick lunch before going to the bank in the afternoon. You have another big day ahead, Kiri, so be prepared. Let's put all these papers into a carrier bag now so you know what to take. Thank goodness you've ordered a taxi. It might be asking for trouble taking this lot on the bus,' said Shelley.

Rupesh phoned that evening. He'd spoken to his father and conveyed the tragic news. His mother was too frail to come to the phone, and his father just kept repeating that this would kill her, this would surely kill her. The parents could not come to England but they'd charged Rupesh with the task of collecting Raja's ashes and returning them to India. They wished to scatter the ashes in one of the sacred rivers of India, as was the Hindu tradition. They did not even speak of Kiri or ask about her wishes.

'I'm sorry they did not ask after you,' Rupesh told Kiri. 'I suspect very little of this was your fault. I know my brother could be very difficult, and I feel sad for you both that you were not accepted as their daughter-in-law.'

'It means a lot to hear you say that, Rupesh. Thank you,' replied Kiri. 'The cremation is arranged for Thursday – that's just two days away. Do I need to delay it until you can come?'

'No. It is better to get these things done quickly. Just keep the ashes safe until I can get there. Will you let me take them back home?'

'Of course I will. It is the right thing, and what would I do with them here where there are no sacred rivers, and no sacred water? There isn't even any sea in Salford.'

Rupesh imagined a rueful smile on her face.

'You are being very brave and gracious, Kiri. I'll phone again when I have made my travel plans and I will see you soon. We wish you well for Thursday and Mandy and I will wake up early to think of Raja and pray at the time of the service.'

29

Mr Black had been wonderfully efficient and already arranged almost everything required to give Raja a fitting send-off. Kiri was so grateful she could have kissed him. All she had to do was approve his decisions and add any personal wishes of her own. She explained a bit about the absence of the Coomaraswamy family.

'Just one thing puzzles me,' said Mr Black, 'Coomaraswamy sounds more like a Sri Lankan name than an Indian name, or am I mistaken?'

'I know what you mean. I think that's why Raja and his brother used the shortened surname of Coomara. I must ask Rupesh more about the name when he comes. Just to confuse you more you'll have noticed I often use my maiden name, which is de Souza. Sri Lanka has many Portuguese influences in its history and I think my ancestors must have come from Portugal. We are quite a mixed-up bunch in Sri Lanka – different religions and origins, and it is the same in India. That is partly why the civil war is raging in our country, with the Tamils who originated in Southern India fighting with the native Sinhalese. It is ruining my beautiful country. Then on top of the war we've had the tsunami. It is all too much – too dreadful to think about.'

'It must be hard for you being so far from your homeland and family at this time,' said Mr Black.

'It is hard, very hard, but I aim to go back to see my mother this year, if I can just get myself together. But one thing at a time – let's get Thursday over and done with first. That will be a tough day. Thank you so much for your help, Mr Black. You have been most kind.'

'It has been my pleasure, Mrs Coomaraswamy.'

Shelley was waiting outside when Kiri emerged from the office.

'How did that go then?' she asked her friend.

'Pretty good actually – I think we are all organised for Thursday. I'll be glad when it's all over,' said Kiri.

'I know,' said Shelley giving Kiri a little hug. 'Come on – let's be off to the solicitors.'

The receptionist at Curtess, French and Bloom showed them into a dark waiting room, furnished with serious mahogany chairs and a central table spread with Country Life magazines and a copy of today's Times. The room smelt musty and portraits of old men in grey suits looked down on them as they waited. Kiri felt small and out of place. Mrs Bloom came out to greet them and showed them into her office, which in contrast was neatly furnished with stylish modern chairs. A vase of white roses brightened the desk.

'Do take a seat. Let me introduce myself – I am Mrs Bloom, the junior partner of Curtess, French and Bloom and I have been allocated to your case.'

Mrs Bloom was an attractive woman, dressed in smart solicitor's attire. Kiri guessed she was in her mid forties and thought how polished and professional she looked in her tailored grey suit, with set golden hair and perfect make-up. It made Kiri feel plain and inadequate in her presence, and she was glad to have Shelley at her side.

'I am sorry for your loss,' continued Mrs Bloom. 'Before we start I'm afraid I must give you our terms and conditions of service. Have a glance at it now, but then please do take it home to read through properly. I must ask you to sign it at the bottom and return it to me in this stamped addressed envelope. Sorry, but we do have to start our business together like that – it's all rather tedious, I know. Now I also have to tell you that the partner who dealt with your husband at the time of your house purchase has himself passed away. But I have had time to look at your file and we still have the conveyancing details here. The good news is that your husband's will is in our archive.'

'Thank you. That is a great relief I must say. We have found no evidence of a will at home,' said Kiri.

Mrs Bloom remained very business-like.

'Right, well I've had a look at it and I can tell you straightaway that you, Mrs Coomaraswamy, are the beneficiary of the house and its contents and your husband's personal effects. The mortgage will be paid off by an endowment policy I believe.'

'That's good news,' said Shelley who had introduced herself simply as Kiri's friend, and not her social worker, much to Kiri's delight.

Mrs Bloom continued, 'Mr Coomaraswamy had two other main assets. The joint bank account will of course come to you, and there was also an investment account in his sole name. The contents of this are to be distributed three ways – one third goes to his parents if he predeceases them, one third will go to his brother, Rupesh Coomaraswamy, and one third will go to a Charmina Patel.'

Kiri's jaw dropped.

30

Kiri and Shelley lunched at Luigi's before their next port of call. Over pasta and salad they discussed the bombshell of the will.

'I can cope with it. I'll still have enough for my own needs and the main thing is that it will eventually get me back to Sri Lanka,' said Kiri. 'If I sell the house and Raja's possessions I think that should provide enough for me to buy a small house to live in with Mama, near Batticaloa. His Rolex watch must be worth a bit to start with, and then there's the furniture. I'll be fine.'

'OK, if that's how you feel, but you could contest the will,' commented Shelley, who had sensed her friend's shock when she heard the name Charmina Patel read out loud.

'He gave me very little when he was alive, and I have no wish to profit further from his death. Charmina was always a shadow in our marriage so I should not have been surprised. We'll see how things go at the bank,' replied Kiri.

'It's a bit early. I fancy some tiramisu and a coffee before we move on. How about you?'

'Why not – all this brain work is bringing my appetite back,' replied Kiri.

At the bank they were shown straight in to see the personal accounts manager, a pert young woman called Miss Osborne. Miss Osborne required proof of identity, and thank goodness the new passport had arrived by post that morning. Kiri produced it from her handbag and dug around in the carrier bag to find the house contents insurance bill, which happily was in joint names, and served as proof of address. This ticked the right boxes for Miss Osborne, who was able to open the account details on screen.

'I can only show you the joint account details. The other account shown at this address does not bear your name I'm afraid. I will have to go through the solicitor to release those details,' reported Miss Osborne.

'I do know about that, and about the contents of the will. Mrs Bloom, my solicitor will be expecting to hear from you,' said Kiri.

'I know Mrs Bloom. We have worked together before, so that's helpful. Now is there anything else I can help you with?'

'I have no cheque book and no cards I can use. Can you arrange these for me?' asked Kiri. 'And I could do with some cash. Can I get money out of the account to keep me going? I will need £100 to pay for incidentals and food until the cheque book comes. Thank you.'

Miss Osborne raised her plucked eyebrows and glanced at Shelley, who nodded in agreement and explained that Raja had dealt with all the household finances, but that Kiri now needed to be able to take over.

'I see. Just fill in this withdrawal form and I'll get some notes for you. I'll be right back.'

Miss Osborne even managed a little smile as she handed ten crisp £10 notes to a grateful Kiri, before they shook hands as they said goodbye.

'We may need to meet again once the will is finalised, so keep in touch and do get back to me personally if I can help with anything else in the meantime. Here's my card,' said the young bank manager.

'Home, James,' announced Shelley when they got to the car.

'Who is James?' asked Kiri, making Shelley laugh again.

They were pleased with how the day had gone and on the way back through the city and out to Salford, Shelley asked if she should inform people who might want to come about the time of the cremation.

'No-one will want to come. It'll just be me, and hopefully you too, and a couple of others perhaps. You will be able to come won't you? Mr Black has ordered a car for me and I wondered if you would come to the house first, to join me in the car. I think I'll be very nervous on Thursday,' said Kiri in a vulnerable voice.

'Of course I'll be there, and there may well be a few others. I'll come to the house about 10 o'clock. Tell me again what you'll be wearing – do I have to wear white too?' asked Shelley.

'No, you wear what you want,' Kiri replied. 'I shall wear my new white blouse and long black skirt, with a long jacket over it. The jacket has a horrible white plastic belt – I think I'll replace it with a black leather belt I have, and add a black silk scarf. That will be respectful and also comfortable.'

'That sounds perfect for the occasion. Do you ever wear a sari? I've never seen you in one,' asked the English friend.

'I used to wear a sari in the summer when I first came to England, but it is too cold in the English winter so I gave them up. I think a cardigan and winter coat spoils the look, don't you? And they are really difficult to fold and put on by yourself. There is no-one to help me with dressing, so that's why I stick to tunics and trousers most of the time. Anyway my saris are looking rather shabby now, and they are very expensive to replace. I still keep two or three old ones in my wardrobe – I haven't the heart to throw them away,' Kiri explained.

'I'd love to see them some time. One day can you show me how to wear one? I've always wondered how they worked.'

'I'll dress you up in one when we have time, but not tonight. I'm too tired after this day of high finance. Next week, after the funeral, come over one evening and I'll cook you a special

Sri Lankan meal to say thank you for all your help. Bring your camera and I'll dress you in a sari, and we can record the moment for posterity.'

'That would be wonderful. It's a deal,' said Shelley. 'Now tomorrow you should have a quiet day getting ready for Thursday. It'll be a difficult enough day without being exhausted too.'

31

Thursday came all too soon. Kiri woke up with an awful wave of anxiety. Her head was tense, and her tummy jittery – she couldn't face breakfast so she just drank sweetened tea for energy. It helped. She dressed in good time and was pleased when she looked in the mirror. She thought she looked quite stylish and modern in the black and white combination, but still appropriate for a grieving widow. She no longer wished to look like the poor oppressed woman she had been when Raja was alive. She wanted to say farewell to him with her head held high, and then step towards her future feeling good about herself.

Shelley arrived just before ten, wearing a trendy grey woollen suit, with a deep purple blouse under it. She had a black wrap around her shoulders instead of a coat.

'Will you be warm enough without a coat?' asked Kiri.

'Stop worrying about me. It's my job to worry about you today. Have you had some breakfast to see you through the morning?' asked Shelley.

'I couldn't eat,' admitted Kiri.

'At least have some fruit. Here – have a banana.' Shelley picked one from the fruit bowl in the kitchen. 'The car will be here soon.'

Kiri felt self-conscious sitting in the back of the big black car with Shelley, as if everyone they passed was peering in at them. They were greeted at the entrance to the crematorium by Mr Black and the priest, and when Kiri walked into the crematorium's chapel she was amazed to see how many people had already taken their seats. Near the front was Mr Thompson, with Angie, his secretary, and a young man who turned out to be his registrar, Jack. Behind him sat Pauline and Andy, and

Dr Anne and Ramona were just across the aisle, in front of a small crowd of Asian men, whom Kiri didn't recognise at all. At the back, and sitting alone, dressed all in black, was an attractive dark-haired woman, who Kiri thought looked just like the woman in the picture in Raja's drawer. She had no time to think about this now, though – she turned to the front of the chapel where the coffin was already in place, and saw a small picture of her late husband on top of it, surrounded by an arrangement of white lilies.

She was disappointed they were not lotus flowers, but you don't get many lotus flowers in Salford. When her time came she would have lotus flowers on her coffin in Sri Lanka, because that was where she wanted to end her life, not here in this cold dark country so far from home.

The ceremony began with much chanting by the priest, and after a while the Asian men joined in. The mantras were soothing, and Kiri got through the next half hour in a sort of trance, unable to understand much of the language used. The priest finished the service with some sentences in English, which was when Shelley grabbed Kiri's hand, and they watched the plain wooden coffin slide slowly away behind a heavy, maroon velvet curtain – the sound of the mechanism discreetly obscured by recorded sitar music.

Mr Black shepherded the mourners out through a side door, where they all hovered, not knowing quite what to do next. There were no tears at this funeral, and just a few kind handshakes, before most of the dutiful congregation drifted away. Kiri looked for the woman in black, but she had slipped away, and so had Jack.

Shelley and Ramona stayed back when Dr Anne returned to work, and with Pauline and Andy they took Kiri to a nearby pub for a drink. Kiri and Pauline were on orange juice, and

Andy had a shandy. Shelley was driving, so ordered a tonic water with ice and lemon, leaving Ramona feeling obliged to have a glass of white wine.

'It'll be a poor celebration of someone's life without a toast,' she said, and they all raised a rather uncertain glass to Raja.

'I don't wish to celebrate his life, or his death,' announced Kiri. 'I just hope he finds more happiness in the next life, and that his reincarnation brings better things for him.'

'That's the most generous thing I have ever heard,' said Shelley, whose eyes became teary as she looked across the table at the dignified little woman who had become her friend. Shelley always had to have a cry at a funeral.

* * *

It was hard over the next few weeks, keeping house alone and having to think of every single thing for herself with little or no help. Kiri found her energy levels flagged easily and her direction in life wavered. Penny phoned regularly and Jean phoned from time to time. Shelley popped in after work when she could and helped with more of the endless forms and paperwork. There was so much to do. But things couldn't be finalised until after the inquest. Kiri felt stuck in some sort of limbo. She did manage to cook Shelley her promised meal and the women got the saris out for inspection, but they never quite got round to dressing up for the photo. Kiri's heart just wasn't in it.

The thing Kiri found most satisfying in these difficult weeks was visiting Pauline and seeing her through her ups and downs. She was happy to stay with her on the bad days as well as the good ones and this helped Andy to get to work. Kiri did bits of personal shopping for Pauline and helped unpack the supermarket delivery when it came – Andy and Pauline had become experts at on-line shopping. On bright days they wrapped up warm and walked to the park, and Pauline showed off her range of hats to the outside world.

Kiri and Pauline loved talking about Sri Lanka and pored over and over Penny's photos from 1978. Pauline kept returning to the one of Mount Lavinia, wondering if she would ever get there. She didn't share with Kiri the thought that it was unlikely. Pauline had two cycles of chemo to go, but she knew that would not cure her, just hold things back for a while.

One day when Kiri was there with Pauline Mrs Woodward called by from the Breakthrough Breast Cancer support group. She was this year's chairperson and was keen to get some fundraising organised so she'd come to follow up Pauline's idea of a fashion show featuring hats and head-scarves. Pauline was under the weather that day, so Kiri stepped in and offered to help as much as she could. Pauline volunteered names of some of her colleagues from the department store who might help and she thought they might even lend outfits for the evening. Kiri suggested the nurses from the breast clinic might be models alongside some patients – she'd ask Ramona to canvass them. Mrs Woodward had already commandeered a small army of volunteers and booked the community hall for an evening just after Easter, when spring would be springing. Pauline's chemo would be finished by then so she might be able to do a demonstration of scarves and tying techniques.

'Would it be too late for an Easter Bonnet competition?' asked Mrs Woodward, who had something of the 'old school' about her.

Pauline wrinkled her nose. 'I'm not sure that's quite my scene, but yes, it would be too late anyway, being after Easter. It might not go down too well with our multi-cultured group, or the younger members either of course.'

'Yes, I suppose we do have some very young members these days. I dare say they might want a bit more pazzazz. OK, thanks for the coffee. I must be off – things to do, people to see,' and the whirlwind that was Mrs Woodward swept out and off down the street, going over lists in her mind as she went.

The fashion show certainly gave Pauline and Kiri something to focus on during the last two cycles of chemotherapy, and Andy was pleased to see his wife involved with something so positive when she was feeling so poorly. She loved showing off her new scarves to him, but he still thought she looked beautiful just plain bald. Pauline used Kiri as a model to experiment on, and enjoyed trying different colours against her smooth brown skin – not milky chocolate, not coffee coloured, but something in between. With her dark brown eyes she looked good in tropical pinks and vibrant reds, as well as turquoise blues and greens. Actually she looked good in most colours, except yellow which seemed colour-draining. Yellow didn't suit Pauline either, and she realised it didn't suit many people – she decided to avoid yellow in the show – it was too much of a challenge for a relatively amateur stylist.

In the middle of all this organising, up came the date for Raja's inquest. Mrs Bloom informed Kiri she was not required to attend in person. The inquest was a formality in the case of any accidental death, mainly to ensure that no foul play was involved. Kiri was pleased to be able to tell Mrs Bloom that she didn't wish to go, and anyway she was very busy. She kept the nagging worry of the frayed seatbelt to herself and as for the knife thoughts – they were best forgotten completely. It may have been careless of him, or even negligent to drive with a faulty seatbelt, but it was his choice.

Three days later Mrs Bloom phoned to say the inquest was over. The police and paramedics had given their reports, and Kiri's statement was read out as was the carpenter's. After due consideration, the verdict was given as 'Accidental Death by Misadventure' and that, she said, was the end of that.

'So now I can get on with settling the estate,' she said. 'I have the addresses for your late husband's parents, but I am having difficulty finding Charmina Patel. I'm sorry to have to ask but do you have any information about her whereabouts?'

'I'm glad the inquest is over and I didn't have to go. Thank you for telling me, but no, I don't know where Ms Patel lives. Her family were from Bangalore and many years ago she lived for a while in Sri Lanka, in Kandy. Rupesh might know more. I can give you his number in Canada.'

'Yes, that would help. I can try him next,' said the solicitor. 'I'll get on to the mortgage company and the bank so they can resolve their accounts, and you, my dear, can dispose of any of your late husband's property from the house if you wish. I know that was your intention.'

'Yes indeed. I will need to raise some cash, even if the house is now mine and the mortgage paid. Shelley is looking into whether I am eligible for any widow's pension from Raja's superannuation too. When I put the house up for sale, can I ask you to help with the conveyancing?' asked Kiri.

'I would be delighted to,' replied Mrs Bloom. 'Now, in case it comes in handy when the time comes I have prepared a list of firms who do house clearances, or take other effects – jewellery, watches and other precious items to be auctioned. Shall I send it to you? You have to be careful to only use reputable agents because there are lots of sharks out there.'

'Yes please, that's just what I need. Thank you so much for all your help. I'll be in touch about the house. Oh, and what about estate agents?'

'I can send a list of those too – local firms you can trust. Goodbye for now, Kiri, and all the best.'

Mrs Bloom got on with phoning Rupesh straightaway. He had an old address in Bangalore for Charmina.

'Who is this woman?' asked Mrs Bloom.

'She was my brother's fiancée before he ran off with Kiri,' he told her. 'It was one of those semi-arranged engagements, but they fell in love with each other. Well, he fell more for her than she for him. She was rather hoity-toity and she tended to look down on Raja, but the parents were all thrilled with the match. When Raja got involved with Kiri, I think Charmina saw it as a way out, and she called the engagement off pretty smartly. The parents were all mortified, and Raja has hardly spoken to our parents since. They never accepted Kiri and made her a scapegoat for my brother's foolishness, but he of course was old enough to know better. I rather liked Charmina, and when she left Kandy and returned to Bangalore and I was travelling, we met up a few times, much to my brother's dismay. Anyway, that's why I kept her address. She got a job on Indian television I think, and she too travelled but kept her base in Bangalore. We lost touch when I went to Canada. I do know that Charmina changed her name for her work – she wanted something that sounded more international, with a bit of show-biz about it. I gather she is now called Charm Diamond. Google that and I think you'll find her.'

'Charm Diamond! What a bizarre choice of name. I'll try it, and thanks for your help,' said Mrs Bloom. She realised Bloom was an odd choice of name too, but then she hadn't exactly chosen the name, just the husband.

'My pleasure,' replied Rupesh, 'And if you need anything else, I shall be coming over to England next week on my way to

India. I am taking Raja's ashes to my parents in India and we will scatter them in the Kaveri River.'

32

A letter from Rupesh arrived, announcing his journey to England, bringing Mandy with him. The children would stay with Mandy's sister for ten days, so as not to miss school. Kiri felt her heart skip a beat when she heard about her niece and nephew – children she had thought very little about until now. The nine year old girl and the seven year old boy were the next generation of her family, even though not related by blood, and she wanted to know more about them. For now she was simply told how excited they were to go to stay with their Canadian cousins. Thank goodness Rupesh and Mandy had booked a room for two nights at the Manchester Hilton, so Kiri didn't have to put them up, and they assured her they would bring photos of the children with them. If they just stayed for two days that would give her plenty of time to prepare for the trip to Essex.

Kiri called the Co-op undertakers to arrange to collect the ashes. She hadn't wanted them in the house until now, but thought she could cope with their presence for just a couple of days until Rupesh and Mandy arrived.

Mr Black answered the phone. 'How are you my dear? I have wondered how you were getting on and when you might be ready to receive the ashes. I was about to write and ask you just that.'

'I'm quite well, thank you, Mr Black, and yes, it is time for the ashes to go home. My brother-in-law is going to take them to Raja's parents in India, where they will be scattered on the river. He tells me he has all the right permissions already.'

'That sounds good. There'll be just one more document from me, which I can give you when you come to collect the casket tomorrow.'

That day Kiri wrote again to Mama, and told her all the news, especially the wonderful hopes she had of getting to know more of her niece and nephew. This was truly wonderful for Lali too, as neither of her sons had produced children. Kiri's oldest brother was almost certainly gay, but this was never spoken of in the family, and the second brother had never got round to marrying, despite an endless string of girlfriends. He was too busy being a play-boy to settle down and have children. It takes all sorts, thought Kiri as she wrote, and at least they have made lives for themselves without getting involved in the civil war back home.

She told her mother she was putting the house on the market, and as soon as the estate was settled she would buy a one way ticket to Sri Lanka. She whispered the last sentence as she wrote it, 'Take care while you wait for me, Mama.'

Mrs Bloom had a busy day too. She was still searching for Charmina, or Charmian, or Charm, or whatever she was now called – the internet was such a useful tool in such cases. She was secretly excited when she found her on the pages of the Indian Star Plus TV channel. There was even a picture of her – strikingly beautiful, mature but certainly glamorous, with glossy black hair and thick eye-liner accentuating her large almond eyes. Wow, thought Mrs Bloom, feeling suddenly matronly in her boring work suit and her short curly hair.

It seemed Charm was an announcer doing the links between programmes, in a deep sultry voice which could be heard on attached video clips. Her life might have been very different if she'd married Raja, she thought, and it doesn't look as if she needs his money – what a shame when poor Kiri could do so much more with it. Mrs Bloom chastised herself for being so judgemental – it wasn't up to her how her clients left their money. She wrote a business-like letter to Ms Charm Diamond, previously known as Charmina Patel, marked'Confidential' and addressed it care of the Star Plus Television station in India. She asked Charm to contact her as soon as possible about a matter which might benefit her.

33

Rupesh and Mandy's visit was easier than Kiri expected. She was very nervous about them coming to her house, which she imagined to look small and dull compared with theirs in Ontario. She'd looked up Ontario during one of her internet lessons with Shelley. It seemed an interesting province, with the vibrant capital city of Toronto alongside one of its southern lakes. It made her think about the lakeside in Kandy, where she had started her adult life, only Toronto was vast and rich, and people like James Taylor and kd Lang sang songs about Toronto and Ontario. Christopher Plummer was born there and so was Bryan Adams – she liked his voice – her mind drifted. She had learned a lot, listening to Radio 2 during her long lonely days at home when Raja was at work.

Anyway Rupesh (call me Ru) and Mandy arrived for tea and cakes on their first afternoon in England. They looked spaced-out with jet lag but were charming and considerate, and didn't overwhelm Kiri at all. Kiri let Ru potter about in Raja's study looking for brotherly memories, while she and Mandy chatted in the living room. Mandy seemed genuinely interested in how Kiri was coping as a widow, and was so pleased her life was filling up with new interests. She heard about the fashion show, and the computer lessons, and how she was going to Essex for a holiday soon. Kiri explained how the Boxing Day tsunami had woken her from a twenty-year sleep, and made her realise she needed to get back to Sri Lanka, even before the death of her husband. Selling this house would now make this possible.

Mandy liked the unassuming Sri Lankan woman and was immediately impressed by her attitude. She suggested they exchange email addresses and write to each other, saying it would be good practice for Kiri's computer skills, as well as allowing her to hear more about her niece and nephew. Mandy brought pictures of the children out of her wallet and proudly showed them to Kiri. The girl was slim, and fair, and suntanned – pretty but unsmiling, embarrassed by the camera, said her mother. The boy was shorter, and darker, and handsome, like his father, with a cheeky grin on his face.

'Shall I email some photos when I get home to Toronto?' asked Mandy.

'That would be wonderful,' said Kiri.

The women were having the same thought when Mandy spoke, 'It's such a shame Raja and Ru didn't get on better. We could have been friends and I could have helped you, albeit from a distance, through the dark times. I think Ru feels guilty too, not just about his brother, but about leaving his parents alone in India. They were pretty authoritarian as parents and in robust health when he left, so it was easy at first – you know, good to get away, but now they are fading he finds it hard. That's why he wants to help now by taking the ashes back to the family home and comforting them. It's the least he can do.'

'Leaving home and changing continents is never easy,' said Kiri, with understanding.

Ru came back to the living room holding a little statue of Ganesha which he'd found on a shelf in the study.

'Do you think I could have this, to remind me of Raja?' he asked.

'Of course, I'd like you to take anything you want from there, and anything you think your parents would like to have. I was just telling Mandy that soon I will sell this house and move back to Batticaloa to be with my mother. Please take as much as you want, or else it will be sold.'

The three of them went into the study and Ru and Mandy chose some bits and pieces to take with them – some books, two small framed paintings of exotic birds which they thought the children might like, and a fine etching of an elephant for the grandparents. Ru chose some gold cufflinks for himself. They weren't sure of the baggage allowance and they still had the casket to take.

Mr Black had sealed the casket and packaged it up, ready for the flight. As Kiri handed it over she thought how strange it felt to be handing over the last remains of the man she had lived with for more than half her life. Mandy and Ru went back to the hotel for much-needed sleep. The next day Ru would call on Mrs Bloom, while Mandy visited an art gallery, then early the morning after they would fly off to India, to deliver Raja home to his parents.

Kiri phoned Penny to tell her about the successful visit from her in-laws. Penny noted a new lightness and enthusiasm for life each time they spoke. She was just like a butterfly developing from a caterpillar, like in the picture book she used to read to Hettie and Theo. She decided to look for the book to show it to Kiri when she came – 'The Beautiful Butterfly' – it must be in the loft somewhere. They chatted about what they'd do when Kiri visited and made arrangements for Penny to come and collect Kiri at the end of the week. She would stay one night and they'd drive back the next day – 250 miles was too much to do a return journey the same day.

Oh gosh, thought Kiri, I've never had a house guest before – another challenge for me, but a pleasant one this time. She'd been planning what to take with her to Essex for ages, but before packing she decided to give the house a thorough spring-clean. She rang Pauline to let her know she would be away for a few days. Pauline was having a good week so she and Andy said they'd look after the spare key and keep an eye on the house for her, in case it fell down in her absence. The humour didn't help – just made Kiri more nervous of leaving.

The big day came and Penny set off on her long journey up the motorways of England, to the north. She enjoyed driving on her own with the radio turned up, swapping between Radio 2 and 5 Live. To ring the changes she had a stack of CDs on board too, and she sang along to these with uninhibited enthusiasm. She had a secret love of motorway service station food and tucked into a steak pie and chips with a lemonade when she felt in need of refreshment. She never ate pies at home and she smiled as she imagined Clive frowning at her and tweaking her waistline – he was so self-disciplined with his own dietary choices, it made her want to rebel sometimes. She went back to the counter and ordered a lemon cheesecake, and coffee. After filling herself up, she filled the petrol tank, and muttered about the escalating price of petrol.

The M6 around Stafford was full of heavy goods vehicles and Penny had to concentrate hard on driving. She wondered what all these lorries were doing on the road late on a Friday afternoon, and where on earth they were all going. She was tired and ready for a strong cup of tea by the time she reached Salford. Kiri showed Penny her room and then the two women popped round to see Pauline to give her the spare key and say cheerio. Penny thought how pale and thin the poor woman looked, despite her cheerful manner. She'd seen that look before and thought Pauline might not be long for this earth. Walking home she tried to talk to Kiri about the prognosis.

'I do know she's not going to be cured, Penny, and that this disease will catch up with her in the end, but for now I can be her friend and help her. None of us know how long she's got, so we must make every week and every day as good as we can. She's so involved in planning the fashion show – I think that's keeping her going at the moment. Her aim is to enjoy that and raise lots of money, and after that it'll be one step at a time. Andy knows too, so don't worry too much,' said Kiri.

Penny loved the fact that the lay person could reassure the GP.

At least three times Kiri had to check the house for unlocked windows and dripping taps before they left the next morning, and they still had to turn back once to check the front door was locked before they hit the road. Kiri enjoyed the changes of scenery as they drove south down the M6, then the M1, before crossing to the east on the A14. She was less impressed with the service station food, and they both settled for salads and fruit during a comfort break. Penny said that Clive would have a meal prepared for them at home – probably a chilli, his signature dish, and usually very tasty.

The Huxtable house was lovely and warm, and welcoming. Kiri liked the eclectic mix of decoration and furnishings, which somehow looked as if it was all meant to go together, even though nothing matched. That shows some skill, thought Kiri – she should have been an interior designer, not a doctor. Clive arrived home from evening surgery and opened a good bottle of Rioja to go with the chilli which he had prepared the night before – to allow the flavour to develop apparently. Kiri felt happy and well in this civilised atmosphere. Penny told her to enjoy the peace – the kids were both out for the evening, but would no doubt liven the place up when they returned.

They had a lovely few days together. They visited the coast at Aldeburgh, walked along the river at Dedham, had afternoon tea in Lavenham, went shopping in Colchester and had a peep at the Castle there. Hettie joined them for everything that included shopping, but Clive and Theo kept out of the way unless food or drink was involved.

When they talked about Kiri's future plans Penny was

impressed at how much thought had gone on. As soon as the solicitor gave her the go-ahead she was putting the house on the market, and if it sold quickly, she planned to rent a small room somewhere until she was ready to go. She had already written to the headmistress of St Mary's School, near Batticaloa, where her mama lived, and the headmistress had provisionally offered her a post as a teaching assistant in the junior school, as well as being a support worker in the nursery school. They wanted her to come in September if possible, for the start of term, and she could live in the dormitory with her mother until they found a house to live in. If she couldn't buy one, she would build one.

'I think I will have enough money from the house sale, especially if I get rid of the contents, and Raja's things. There may well be some money left over and I've been thinking of starting a small charity to help with the school's rebuilding projects, and the orphans in the Batticaloa district. What do you think?' asked Kiri.

'What a brilliant idea, but it would be hard work. Have you spoken to anyone about it?' said Penny.

'Only Mrs Bloom – she's put me in touch with a lawyer who specialises in charities, and I'm meeting with her next week. She says I will need trustees and I thought I might ask you and Jean to help with that, and perhaps Shelley. Andy might join as a treasurer – he does the books at his furniture store. That would be a start wouldn't it?'

'Gosh, it's ambitious, Kiri, but of course I'll help in any way I can. From my experience of charity committees and charity work, I'd say keep it small and personal, and get good legal advice, especially about the overseas aspect. Also if you avoid paid workers and employees you don't have to get tied up with employment law, which can be such a nightmare for small concerns. The main thing is to make sure any money gets properly invested and used for its intended purpose – the school and the children. I'm sure the lawyer will help you draw up terms. It's actually rather exciting isn't it? Let's phone Jean now.'

Soon it was time for Kiri to go home. Clive drove this time in his Saab, with Hettie in the front and Penny and Kiri in the back. Theo opted to stay with a school friend for a couple of days. Hettie was going to university to study architecture in October, and had been offered places at both Leeds Metropolitan and Brighton. After her A levels she went to the local institute to do an Art Foundation Year, and as long as she completed this, her offers were safe. The trouble was she couldn't decide which uni to choose. Each of the courses had its own advantages, and it all boiled down to which city she'd rather live in, so the opportunity of another trip to Leeds to look round seemed a good idea.

'Thank you so much for a lovely holiday,' said Kiri, 'Just come in for a minute before you set off – there's something I want to give you. She went into the study and reappeared, carrying a roll of fabric. She unfurled it carefully to reveal a beautiful embroidered hanging that she had made during those lonely days in the house. It was worked in a myriad of red, brown and gold threads on a dappled dark green batik background, depicting abstract animal shapes and birds in a forest landscape. It was finished but not mounted or framed.

'With your stylish eye and skills as an interior designer, Penny, do you think you can make something out of this? I would like you to have it and try,' said Kiri.

'Did you do this? It's wonderful – so rich, with amazing depth of colour. It almost looks three-dimensional. It must be seventy centimetres wide, and so detailed and intricate. However long did it take you? Hettie, come and look at this,' called Penny.

‘Wow, that’s amazing,’ said the girl. ‘For us? Mum, it would look great, protected in a recessed dark wooden frame. It would go perfectly in our hallway, wouldn’t it?’

‘It really would – yes, it’s a lovely gift. Are you sure, Kiri? We’ll certainly look after it and display it proudly. Thank you. Now come on young lady,’ said Penny turning to Hettie, ‘we must be off or we’ll miss seeing the university in daylight hours.’

34

Mrs Bloom's letter found its way to Charm Diamond at her apartment in Mumbai, having been forwarded from the Star Plus Television offices. Charm, as she now called herself, kept a holiday home in Bangalore, the Garden City of India, to be near her family, but spent most of her working life on the road or in Mumbai. She had become a well-known figure on Indian TV, but as she got older she spent less time in front of the camera and more time as a producer and director. She had an affluent lifestyle as an independent woman in Mumbai, and frequented the best parties and dinners in town. She managed to keep her personal life surprisingly private considering her high profile. In her thirties she'd had a failed marriage to an Indian actor and hated the intrusion of the press at that awful time when her life was in tatters, so since then she'd vowed to keep herself and her relationships private. She'd also started to work hard on a change of image, but was finding it hard to shake off the glamour girl label. Her glitzy past haunted her now she wanted to be considered a serious broadcaster and she felt the public could be very unforgiving.

Charm read the letter from England with suspicion. It might be from a bounty hunter, or the press trying to get through to her, and she did not need this right now. She was just at the start of a promising new relationship with a writer of some acclaim, and was trying to consolidate the idea that she was a serious and intelligent player in the world of broadcasting. Still there was something intriguing about a letter from Salford, Greater Manchester, UK and she wondered what on earth it could be about. Charm decided a cautious reply from her work email address was the safest option. She and Mrs Bloom entered into a series of email exchanges, each explaining their positions until they trusted one another well enough to have a phone conversation.

'Miss Diamond, we speak at last,' said the capable Mrs Bloom. 'You are now aware that you have been left a considerable sum from the estate of Mr Raja Coomaraswamy, and I require proof of identity and your bank details so I can make the money transfer. I will of course need a mailing address for the paperwork and I will then need you to sign a written receipt.'

'Thank you, Mrs Bloom, but as I have already intimated, I neither want, nor need any money from Mr Coomaraswamy. He has been out of my life for over twenty years and I cannot think why he has left me money in his will. It all seems quite bizarre – I thought he had a wife and family,' replied Charm.

'He had a wife, and she has been looked after, as have his parents who are still alive, but sadly he and his wife had no children.'

'Oh, I thought... never mind,' said Charm. 'Please just give the money to his widow.'

'I cannot do that. I am obliged by the terms of the will to give the money to you, and it is then up to you what you do with it. You could contact the widow yourself or give the money to a deserving charity if you wish, but I must give it to you first of all.'

'I see. I understand your position. Send it to me then and I will give it some more thought. Are you allowed to give me Mrs Coomaraswamy's address please?' asked Charm.

Mrs Bloom hesitated, 'I'll have to ask her permission for that. Do I have your permission to pass on your address in return?' she replied.

'You may give her my office address, but not my home one. I do try to keep that private.'

'I quite understand, Miss Diamond. We'll get on with all this immediately. Thank you for talking to me. Goodbye,' said Mrs Bloom with some relief. This extended family was the weirdest and most complex she'd come across for quite a while. Still, she thought, it spiced up the working day somewhat, talking to people from all over the world and television stars at that. Whoever said life in a small firm of solicitors would be too dull for her?

35

Mrs Woodward didn't like to phone Pauline in case she was resting, so Kiri became their go-between, and Mrs Woodward was on the line almost daily about the fashion show as the date grew nearer. Kiri had a key to Pauline's house so could let herself in without disturbing her – Pauline seemed to need more and more rest, and Andy was pleased that Kiri was there so much. He tried to get to work most days, even though he often went in late, or brought paperwork home. With one week to go plans were in place for the big event. Pauline had just finished her last cycle of chemo and should be on an 'up' week. The models were chosen, along with the outfits and accessories – hats and scarves matched up. The posters had been displayed for some weeks, and over a hundred tickets had been sold for £5 each. Pauline had allowed a raffle to take place, but no Easter Bonnet competition. Tea and coffee with home-made biscuits, courtesy of Mrs Rees, the surgeon's wife, would be available at the interval, and the music for the catwalk show was provided by Ramona's boyfriend, who ran a mobile disco. The catwalk itself was made by the warehousemen from Andy's furniture store. It was a real team effort.

Andy drove Pauline and Kiri to the community centre in good time, and all the helpers got a little pep talk from Mrs Woodward before the guests arrived. The hall filled up with a buzz of excitement and the music started. Women of all shapes and sizes, colours and creeds, young and old, paraded up that catwalk in order to raise money for Breakthrough Breast Cancer. The finale of the catwalk show was Kiri modelling a beautiful sari, with a toning headscarf, draped and folded expertly by Pauline to give it some height, and pinned with a beautiful encrusted brooch. The sari was a flattering deep turquoise silk and Kiri glowed: she felt fabulous.

After the interval Pauline gave a demonstration of different ways to use scarves – revealing her secrets on how to tie and drape them to best effect. The bra fitting team made a generous donation to the charity and in return were allowed to set up a stall in an ante-room, where they were available for consultations and sales. At the end of the evening Mrs Woodward drew the raffle. Andy won a bottle of champagne and Ramona won a make-over at a nearby beauty salon. After all the prizes had been given Mrs Woodward thanked everyone for coming to what had been a most successful evening, and gave special thanks and a bouquet of flowers to Pauline, whose idea it was. The amount raised for charity would be announced in the gazette next week.

Pauline and Andy were both exhausted that night and slept better than they had for months, but Pauline had to stay in bed the next day too, and the day after that. She felt weak and sick, and Andy hoped she had just overdone it at the fashion show. When she didn't pick up over the next few days he asked the GP to visit. Dr Dixon called in on her rounds, and noted that Pauline had a yellow tinge in her eyes. She took various blood samples including liver function tests, and said she'd have a talk with Pauline's Macmillan nurse, Sadie. She left a prescription for some gentle anti-nausea tablets and instructions to drink plenty of clear fluids.

That was the beginning of a downhill spiral for Pauline, who never did pick up. The Macmillan nurse was wonderful at controlling her pain and keeping her comfortable, and she and Dr Dixon visited regularly. Pauline made one more visit to Oncology outpatients for specialist review, and it was decided by all concerned that the cancer was spreading too fast now, and the main aim was to keep Pauline comfortable. Tears were shed, and Andy arranged compassionate leave from work. Kiri went round often, to give Andy a break and allow him time to get out of the house for brief spells, but she was careful not to invade their privacy. Pauline's parents and sister came and went and came back again, not knowing quite what to do with themselves.

Pauline remained remarkably calm. She said all the things she needed to say to the people she loved, and was asleep more than she was awake. When she could no longer take tablets and was in need of pain relief for her swollen liver and back pain, the district nurses set up a syringe-driver which slowly injected a painkiller, and that made her more peaceful. Pauline had discussed her preferred place of care with Dr Dixon and Sadie and said she would like to die at home, in her own bed, with her family nearby – and one Wednesday, in the early hours of the morning, that's just what happened. Andy and her mum sat at Pauline's bedside after she'd passed, until Dr Dixon arrived at 8 o'clock to certify the death. Dr Dixon had seen many scenes of grief before, but still was moved by the love she witnessed in this close-knit family, and had to blink away her own tears as she tried to bring them some comfort. Then she had to walk away and get on with her working day. She told them the death certificate would be available to collect from the surgery by lunchtime, and invited Andy to make an appointment to come talk to her at the surgery whenever he needed.

Sadie arrived just as Dr Dixon was leaving and took over, talking the family through the next steps. She phoned the funeral director for Andy but he insisted on phoning Kiri himself, knowing she would be waiting for the call. Kiri felt the ache of loss, deep within her when she put the phone down. She wept more than she had when her own husband had died, and even though she was prepared for this death, it affected her greatly. Over the forthcoming days she found herself not wanting to go out again, and hiding away at home, feeling lost and sad.

Shelley saw this reaction, and stepped up her presence in Kiri's life, concerned that her friend would return to her old negative ways and never get back to Sri Lanka. The computer lessons had lapsed when Pauline was so ill, so Shelley suggested they resume their attack on the world of information technology. This made Kiri think once more about her own charity – she seemed to benefit from having a project to latch on to and establishing her charity for the school in Sri Lanka was the ideal project. She still thought about Sri Lanka and her mother but it had taken a back seat when she was with Pauline. They met the charity lawyer, who gave them the advice they needed, and now she and Shelley worked together on a mission statement and a business plan.

36

Kiri prepared herself for the second funeral in four months, and the two events couldn't have been more different. Pauline's farewell took place in her family church in Knutsford. It was only 16 miles away and cars from Salford were arranged for friends who needed transport. Pauline had been a choirgirl at this church and the rector knew all her family well, so the service had a very personal feel to it. He spoke warmly about Pauline and recalled her joyful marriage to Andy nearly six years ago at which he had been honoured to officiate. He praised Andy for his unstinting love and support for Pauline during their all too short time together as man and wife. The church was full of family and friends, old and new, and through their tears the congregation sang Pauline's favourite hymns with surprising gusto. An old school friend read a lovely poem about remembering, by Christina Rossetti, with only the softest crack in her strained voice, and Kiri wondered how she had managed to speak at all – her own throat was as tight as a knotted rope.

After the service in church family and close friends were invited to go to the crematorium nearby for Pauline's final journey. Andy asked Kiri to go with them if she could manage it. It was only a short time since she had said goodbye to Raja, with all the mixed emotions that brought, but she did manage it – it was the least she could do for Pauline, her good friend.

Tea and tiny sandwiches had been arranged at an old-fashioned hotel opposite the church, and here they all gathered after the cremation to exchange stories and memories of Pauline. Shelley noticed that Kiri looked drained of colour and exhausted by grief, so after a little refreshment she offered to take Kiri home. In front of the house when she dropped her off Shelley saw a new For Sale sign attached to the garden wall.

'It's on the market, Kiri. Why didn't you tell me?' asked Shelley.

'There's been so much going on here lately hasn't there? I won't pretend it slipped my mind, but other things seemed more important,' replied Kiri.

'I know,' said Shelley. 'When you need some help with more house clearing, let me know, but meanwhile we'd better get on with the charity too. We need to get working.'

37

Kiri's new computer skills were an enormous benefit because now she could keep useful records of all their deliberations and discussions. After weeks of hard work, with endless meetings and emails, they finally got the charity registered. Trustees were appointed and Shelley was made chairperson of the board. Andy became treasurer, and Pauline's sister, Holly became secretary, while Kiri was honorary president, and designed a simple logo for their letterhead. The logo was based on the shape of the island of Sri Lanka, with a stylised elephant at its centre, holding a pearl in its trunk, and carrying a small child on its back. Kiri just loved elephants, and Sri Lanka was known as the Pearl of the Indian Ocean, so she'd named her charity Pearls across the Sea. They could change it to a more catchy name later if need be, or just shorten it to 'Pearl'.

Visitors to view the house were few and far between and Kiri felt frustrated thinking it might never sell at this rate. When she wasn't working on the charity she plodded on, sifting through things in the house and throwing out as much superfluous rubbish as possible, turning over and over the last vestiges of her married life. She put stuff into piles – one for recycling, one for the hospice shop, one for saving, one for the tip and one to sell to the house clearance firm. She made an appointment for Hoopers, the house clearance people, to come to give her an estimate. She thought she'd like someone with her for this in case she was duped or they took advantage of her lack of business acumen, but Shelley was busy with a big case conference that week and Andy was back at work. Kiri took the plunge and phoned Mrs Woodward.

'I'd be delighted to chaperone you my dear,' boomed Mrs Woodward down the phone-line. 'I promise I won't interfere. I'll just be there to keep an eye on things. I worked for an antique dealer once, so this is right up my street.'

'I don't think you'll find any antiques here, but there may be odd bits of value. Raja had a good eye for furniture,' said Kiri.

'See you at 11 o'clock on Thursday my dear. What fun,' and she was off.

Kiri packed up Raja's clothes in plastic bags and sent the better things to the Hospice and the older things to the Salvation Army. Andy borrowed a van from work and delivered the bags for her, then took various loads to the tip, so when the assessor from Hoopers came he could see the wood for the trees.

Mrs Woodward watched over the man as he scrutinised each and every item – a gold fountain pen, an onyx paperweight, a leather desk set and briefcase, silver cufflinks x 2, watches x 3 – one of which a nice Rolex (who needs three watches?thought Kiri), and then he checked shelf after shelf of books. They moved on to the kitchen items and then furnishings. They counted rugs and stools and chairs and tables and bookcases downstairs. Upstairs they added beds and chests of drawers, bed-side tables, mirrors and wardrobes to the list. This was proving to be a huge job. Kiri kept her own bedroom door closed. She wasn't ready to have her personal things trawled through yet, but knew even they would need to be culled before she could leave.

The assessor said he would put his estimate in writing, and recommend which items should go to auction and which could be purchased directly by his firm, then off he went. Mrs Woodward had thus far remained spookily quiet despite her studious observation of the man. She suddenly piped up,

'Wasn't that fascinating, seeing how they work?' she remarked. 'And you didn't really need my help at all, but I was of course happy to be here. If the money is going to your Pearl charity I think as much as possible should go to auction – you'll make more money that way. But before that I wonder if I could make you an offer for that dear little side table and bookcase in your late husband's study? They would go beautifully in my new extension.'

Kiri had noticed the assessor had been particularly interested in these two mahogany pieces.

'Do you mind if I wait for the valuations first, Mrs Woodward? I think that would be best, and then we'll talk again.'

Kiri realised her business acumen was just fine. Showing the man from Hoopers round the house had been quite fun, but she did hate showing prospective house buyers round. After the first two people took no interest in the house and were actually rather rude, she asked the estate agent to do the showing and she made herself scarce when others came to view. Perhaps the estate agent would do a better selling job than she could.

38

Kiri's three-month check at the breast clinic went well enough, but it made her feel sad to think of Pauline when she walked in. She was cheered to see a notice stuck on the pin board in the waiting area announcing that the fashion show had raised £899 for the Breakthrough Cancer Charity. How pleased Pauline would have been with that total – she must remember to phone Andy to congratulate him when she got home. Poor man must be feeling lost, but at least he was now involved with Pearl and that'll mean we'll keep in touch when I leave, thought Kiri. Leaving seemed another step nearer as she went through her check-up and consultation with Dr Anne.

'You are doing really well, Kiri,' said the good doctor. 'We are very pleased at how well you've settled on the tablets. I do hope you will stay on them for at least two years. Do I gather you hope to be moving away soon?'

'Thank you, yes,' replied Kiri. 'Things are going ahead and soon I will have sold the house. I'd like to be in Batticaloa for the start of term in September.'

'The most we can give you is a six months' supply of medication, so we hope you can get more when you move to Sri Lanka. Now, we've made some checks and the Eastern University Hospital in Batticaloa has a good breast unit. They should be able to take over your care. We've made up a pack for you containing copies of our records, with mammograms and scans, along with our contact details for you to pass to your new clinic – it means they can get in touch if they want any further information.'

'You are so kind. I thank you with all my heart,' said Kiri. 'I will miss you all very much, but Shelley will be keeping in touch and I'm sure she'll let you know how I'm getting on.

She's helping me with my children's charity.'

'Yes, we've heard all about it and it sounds wonderful. I think we were all stunned by the pictures we've seen of the tsunami, and the damage it caused. There must be so many needy children there. I really do wish you well, Kiri. You have become one of our star patients,' said Dr Anne as she escorted Kiri back to the waiting area. Ramona and Shelley came out of their rooms to say goodbye, and all the waiting patients thought there had been a royal visit to the clinic that day.

When she got home the red light was flashing on the ansaphone. The estate agent had left a message asking her to call back as soon as possible. Kiri felt a little flutter of excitement in her heart beat as she dialled the number. A couple who had viewed the house two days earlier had made a good offer on the house, and wanted to come back that afternoon at 4 o'clock for another look.

Kiri scurried around tidying the house and sprucing up the bathrooms. This time she stayed to meet the couple who might be taking over her home. The house smelt of lavender furniture polish and air freshener when the prospective buyers walked in, and both husband and wife looked happy as they wandered around for a second time. He tapped the walls and got out his metal measuring tape, making notes, while his wife looked more closely at the kitchen facilities and the carpets and curtains. The couple were both teachers, and had two growing children so they needed more space than they had in the two-bedroomed terraced house they'd bought when first married. They wanted to be able to give each child a room of its own and a bigger garden for them to play in. The wife wanted a new fitted kitchen, so they'd offered a little under the asking price, but they did want to keep the carpets, which they would pay for separately. A formal offer was made on the house and

Kiri was pleased to hear that they were part of a short chain, so hopefully things would progress smoothly. Kiri could imagine this nice family being happy in the house and was content to accept their offer. She could hardly believe it – she had sold her home and could soon use the money to fulfil her dream. That night she wrote to Mama and told her their reunion was getting closer.

The endless task of house clearing was going well and Shelley often called in to help with that, as well as the charity work.

'When I leave I'd like you to keep the computer as a gift,' said Kiri one day. 'You said yours at home was quite old, and this one is a good model I believe, and it still has some life left in it. I'd be so pleased if you would accept it.'

'I couldn't possibly take it. It's too much,' Shelley replied.

'Well, I can't pack it up and take it with me, and they don't sell on the second-hand market. All the Pearl charity stuff is on it so it'll save transferring it. You can get a computer buff to clear the hard drive of all Raja's rubbish and my personal stuff, then it'll be all yours.'

'I see you've got it all worked out – put like that, how can I refuse? You've become quite the IT expert recently, Kiri. Thanks you very much – I guess I accept,' conceded Shelley, giving her friend a big hug.

'I would like to make you an offer in return though – when you finally leave your house and are waiting to fly off to warmer climes, I want you to come and stay in my spare room. I can't have you in rented accommodation, all alone in a B and B or a house full of strangers. It'll be easier for you to still have some sort of home for your last days in England.'

'I'd love that if you can manage to have me. Thank you,' replied Kiri. 'You're a good friend and an excellent IT teacher, and I shall miss you very much. I do hope one day you'll visit me in Batticaloa.'

'You bet I will. I want to see that school, and if you do build a nursery as you've suggested, then I want to be at the grand opening. How are communications going with the school anyway?' asked Shelley.

'The Board of Governors is very interested in the prospect of a charity specifically to support the residential side of the school and a nursery, so we are keeping in touch. The Chair of the Board has agreed to come on to the Pearl trustee team, and he's going to introduce me to a well-respected business man who he thinks will help us. We will need some local people involved once I get there, but meanwhile Mrs Bloom is being really helpful with the long-distance legalities.'

'Oh, Kiri, it's all coming together so well, you must be excited,' said Shelley.

'Yes, and the main school is doing well with government compensation money to help with the classrooms, but the dormitories and nursery do need our input urgently. I need to get there as soon as possible now to keep up the impetus. I'm phoning Penny tonight because she is hoping to travel with me when I first return. Now the house has sold we plan to book our flights for the first week in September, and mine will be a one way ticket,' Kiri announced with a smile.

When Kiri made the call she found that Penny had already arranged to take the first two weeks of September off work as annual leave, with Clive's blessing, so she was free to accompany Kiri and help her settle in.

'I can't wait to go back there,' Penny told her. 'I can almost smell the warm, spicy, tropical air as I speak. I've never been to Batticaloa of course – the only time Jean and I went to the east coast was for a weekend trip to Trincomalee. It was beautiful there before the civil war. I guess it still might not be safe up there, but hopefully we should be alright in Batticaloa.'

'Yes, Mama says most of the fighting is in the north now, but everyone still has to be careful. I'm sure we'll be fine at the school. So, if you can book the tickets on line I'll send you a cheque for mine when we know the price. I've kept enough money in my current account, and of course my ticket will only be one way.' Kiri rather enjoyed making that point again.

'Let's get on with it, two tickets from Heathrow to Colombo, here we come – then only one ticket to return. What a shame Jean can't get off work this September, but I know she'll be out to see you in the New Year,' said Penny.

39

Exchange of contracts and completion on the house sale was set for mid-August. Hoopers sold Kiri's valuables at auction for more than estimated, and deposited a healthy sum in Kiri's already bulging bank account. The money from the house sale was divided in two by the solicitors and half went into Kiri's personal savings account and half went into the Pearl charity account which had been set up by Andy. He'd done his research as treasurer and, along with advice from Mrs Bloom about any tax liabilities, Kiri was advised it could easily be transferred to a Sri Lankan bank account when the time came.

One week before she was due to move in with Shelley, Kiri received an extraordinary and unexpected letter, with an Indian postmark on the envelope. She opened it with more than a little trepidation and had to read it two or three times before she understood its contents.

Dear Kiri,

I hope you don't mind that I address you informally, and I hope that you are not offended by my making contact with you directly. Firstly I wish to send you my sincere condolences on the death of your husband, Raja. Your solicitor, Mrs Bloom informed me of his death and the contents of his will, which shocked and surprised me, as you may imagine.

I can assure you that I have had no contact with your husband in the last 25 years. I do not wish to benefit from his death in any way, and I feel I do not deserve, want, or need his money. However Mrs Bloom has been legally obliged to send me that which was apparently owed to me, and I have accepted it, but only in order to pass the money on to a suitable charity.

You may know that these days I am involved in the television industry in India. This industry already has a long-standing commitment to a national children's charity based here in Mumbai, so I plan to give some of the money to this worthwhile cause. I have heard from Mrs Bloom that you have founded a charity yourself, to help the orphaned children in your home town of Batticaloa, and I would very much like to donate a substantial sum to your charity.

If you can accept my offer please let me know, along with your charity's bank details, and I will send a bankers draft to you. In return I will require a receipt and as time goes by I'd like an account of how the school project is progressing. I am told you plan to fund a dormitory and a nursery there, and I would appreciate more details in due course, either from you or via Mrs Bloom.

Yours sincerely

Charm Diamond (formerly known as Charmina Patel)

Kiri was astonished. In fact she was even more surprised than when she'd heard about the will for the very first time in Mrs Bloom's office. This woman sounded very convincing. Now she needed to talk to Mrs Bloom about how to reply.

Mrs Bloom admitted she knew what was coming and reassured Kiri that it was all above board, and the money could be gratefully accepted on behalf of the charity. Kiri decided to keep her reply short and business-like.

Dear Charm,

I thank you for your most unexpected letter. After discussion with the trustees of my charity I would be most grateful to accept your donation. We will send you an official receipt once the funds are received. I enclose the appropriate bank details. We will of course let you know about the development of St Mary's School and its nursery and dormitory block which we hope will be officially opened in the New Year.

I am leaving England shortly, so please make further contact through Mrs Bloom, my solicitor and charity trustee, at least until I have a postal address in Sri Lanka.

With kind regards

Kiri de Souza (formerly known as Mrs Kiri Coomaraswamy)

40

Kiri walked out of her Salford house for the last time with wobbly legs and a strange sensation in her chest. There was a leaden lump beneath her breast bone and she had an odd, empty feeling. She was excited but terrified at the same time and had to dig her fingernails into the palms of her clenched hands in an attempt to maintain control. Shelley loaded her into the car with all her bags and they drove off in silence.

For the next two and half weeks Shelley's spare room became Kiri's sanctuary, and she tried not to be a nuisance to her generous friend. She helped with the pets, kept the house tidy, and cooked some of their meals while Shelley continued to go to work. Penny and Kiri spoke daily on the phone making their final arrangements, and Lali de Souza prepared for the arrival of her long-lost daughter in Batticaloa with mounting anticipation.

When Lali was anxious she cleaned, and by the end of the month St Mary's school was dirt-free, neat and tidy. She made up a small bed next to her own, sharing the same mosquito net which hung from the wooden ceiling like a wedding veil. Headmistress had ordered nets for all the beds and had got the laundry up and running, insisting that clean sheets led to clean minds. She was getting order back into the place, but space was still a problem and a new dormitory was much needed. Headmistress was intrigued to be able to soon meet her cook's daughter – a remarkable woman by all accounts and one who she hoped would bring new energy to her school as well as new funds.

Andy drove Kiri to Heathrow when the day of departure finally came. They drove through the pale early morning light which gave the journey a dream-like quality. They'd struggled to get two huge suitcases and one large piece of hand luggage into the car boot – what little to show for the last twenty-odd years, thought Kiri. They met Penny and Clive in the check-in hall, then after hugs and farewells from the men, Kiri and Penny went through security. For the next two hours they were held in that weird transition zone that a departure lounge involves. Penny thought it provided a buffer between one world and the next. They felt in suspended animation – not interested in the duty-free, or food outlets, but simply keen now to get away.

'I'm off to buy some flight socks,' Penny announced. 'I'll bring you some too.'

Kiri's heart lurched when the flight was called. Thank goodness Penny reappeared just in time, and the two women struggled into their tight compression socks.

'Last time I flew was twenty-five years ago,' gasped Kiri, as she sat up, feeling hot with the effort. 'We didn't have flight socks back then. Oh dear.'

'I know,' said Penny. 'You'll be alright. Just stick with me and relax. We'll be fine once we're off. Remember, this is what you've been waiting for all this time.'

'I couldn't do this on my own. Thank you so much for coming with me,' said Kiri.

'I wouldn't have missed it for the world,' said Penny.

The flight was long and they made themselves as comfortable as possible. Hour after hour they sat, twiddling their ankles like fidgety children. Kiri read and Penny snoozed, in between interruptions for drinks, and plastic meals, and films on the in-flight entertainment system. They didn't know if they were eating lunch, dinner or breakfast as those hours dragged by – one meal merged into the next. Their belts felt tighter and so did the flight socks.

At last the captain announced that soon they would be landing in Colombo, where the weather was fine and the temperature a sunny 35 degrees. Kiri gripped Penny's hand hard for the landing. She was back on home soil again, and she said a little prayer of thanks to the Lord Buddha.

'Let life begin again,' she whispered, and the rock that had seemed stuck in her chest for months slowly began to dissolve.

41

They stepped out into the hot Sri Lankan air and the glorious smell of the place attacked their senses. It was a sensation Kiri would never forget and she felt it replenish her soul and her body. Penny and Kiri were battling their way through security and customs when Kiri was stopped and questioned sternly about her reasons for entering Sri Lanka. A gruff customs officer demanded she open her suitcases, with a suspicious, nasty look on his face. He led her into a cubicle and said he would call in a female colleague to do a body search. Kiri started to panic – surely they couldn't refuse her entry to her own country? She pleaded with the man to let her get on with her journey and her voice became shrill with anxiety. Penny was left outside the cubicle and became concerned when she heard raised voices, so she knocked on the door of the little room. She calmly asked if she could help. The customs man spoke good English,

'And who do you think you are? Get out. This is not your business. Your papers are in order. We need to question your friend and sort out some discrepancies.'

'What discrepancies are you talking about?' pursued Penny. 'This lady has been unwell and I am a doctor escorting her back to her family home. She should not be exposed to stress in her condition. May I stay with her while you complete your checks?'

'Huh! Yes, you may stay if Ms de Souza wishes your company, but just as an observer. Please do not interrupt us,' replied the man a little more gently. He didn't want this Sri Lankan woman to lose control in her state of panic and make his tedious job even harder. He turned back to Kiri.

'Ms de Souza, your papers state that your married name was Coomaraswamy, and that you are now widowed. Is that correct? Tell me about your late husband's connection with the Tamil Tigers Support Group in Manchester.'

It dawned on Kiri that this might be why she was being questioned. They suspected some sort of link with terrorism because she had been married to a Tamil, albeit an Indian Tamil – would Raja continue to control her from his grave? She had to defend herself or they might arrest her. Penny watched in admiration as her friend spoke up.

'My husband had no political allegiances known to me,' she announced firmly. 'Yes, he was a Tamil by birth, but he was too busy with his work as a surgeon to get involved with such a group, and I myself am Sinhalese. The civil war is only of interest to me because I mourn the loss of life it has caused. I am not a political animal. I am here to help the children of this country, whatever their religion, their race, or the politics of their parents. Here are the details of my charity, which has been formed to help all children orphaned or damaged by the tsunami. I am for peace, not war.'

After a rudimentary body search for poor Kiri (who had managed to mouth a silent 'sorry' to Penny), they were joined by a senior immigration officer who seemed more reasonable than the rough customs man. Kiri repeated her story to him, and answered more questions, with Penny by her side. They wouldn't even give her a glass of water. She was horrified to learn that Raja had indeed been making donations to the Tamil Group through his friend, Mohan. The questioning went on for two exhausting hours and then suddenly was over. They finally accepted her statements and her lack of involvement in any of Raja's business and the women were free to go.

In the taxi to the Galle Face Hotel Kiri breathed deeply and started to relax again.

'Well, thank goodness that's over. I hadn't expected that,'

announced Kiri.

'Me neither,' said Penny. 'We are here at a strange time for this country. I guess they have to be careful, and we have to have our wits about us.'

They felt disorientated and out of place as they settled into a smart double room at the hotel for their first night in Sri Lanka, and they unpacked the luggage which had been disordered by the customs officer. Before supper they went outside for a walk in the balmy evening air, not daring to go too far before returning to the restaurant for a light meal. Penny felt nauseous with fatigue and jet lag, but managed to send an email to Clive before bed, telling him they had at last arrived safely, and that she loved him very much. She spared him the details of the interrogation – it would only worry him and anyway it would wait for another day.

The next morning they woke early and each took lovely long showers, making the most of the beauty products in the hotel bathroom. At breakfast they could only cope with tea and toast before heading for the station to find the train to Batticaloa. Penny had booked first class tickets, remembering how crowded the second and third class carriages had been twenty-seven years ago, and they were more than grateful for the comfy seats on the nine hour train journey ahead of them. The porters struggled with Kiri's huge cases.

'What have you got in here, love? Sure it's not a dead body?' they joked in Sinhalese.

Kiri shrugged her shoulders and smiled at the good-hearted men before translating for Penny. The porters brought bottles of chilled water and the hotel had packed them a light lunch, which they dipped into as they rumbled across the country to the east coast, gazing through the window at the changing landscape.

42

The train chugged into Batticaloa's main station at evening-time, just as the large orange sun was sinking. They found a large enough taxi to take them, with all their luggage, to St Mary's School and in the fading light Kiri found she could hardly recognise her home town. There were so few trees and so much more traffic than she expected. Many buildings had simply disappeared, whilst others she didn't recognise stood out, some old, some new, some damaged, some intact. As they approached the coast road Kiri could see how much had been lost in the tragedy just nine months ago. They turned a corner towards the school and saw the faithful old banyan tree standing at the roadside, with its multiple trunks and trailing roots and branches. It had clung on, immoveable and strong as the waters came, and remained a sign of continuity and comfort for the people of the town to this day. Kiri had stood under that tree as a child, waiting for the school bus to take her home after lessons were over.

A little welcome party was waiting for them in the school canteen. Across the door a colourful banner was hung saying 'WELCOME KIRIBABA' which Lali had asked the children to help her make. When she saw the taxi approach, Lali called out and girls and women came running from all directions to greet the newcomers, almost displacing Lali from the front of the queue for hugs and kisses. Kiri found Mama and Mama found Kiri, and they clung to each other, unable to speak, as the small crowd thronged round them. Penny looked on with tears rolling down her face, and a small girl sidled up next to her and slipped her hand into hers, then reached up to pat Penny's face dry with the other hand.

After the first rush of emotion they settled down to

introductions. Kiri and Penny were introduced in English to Headmistress and some of the teachers and girls who resided in the cramped dormitory with Lali. They were plied with refreshments – rice, vegetables and fruit with drinks of tangy lime juice. Penny had loved lime juice for twenty-seven years and the perfume of it always took her back to Sri Lanka in her mind. It switched on her salivary glands as she supped happily on the wonderful sharp nectar. It made her shiver, like eating sherbet. They had slices of mango and papaya, which tasted nothing like the bland things you got in British supermarkets – flavour sapped and wasting the air-miles – here they were like heavenly bursts on the taste buds and Penny had to restrain herself from being too greedy. Kiri was too busy talking to eat, and sat holding her mama's hand as if she would never let go.

Penny was tired and soon excused herself, to go and find her hotel. Headmistress sent her in the rusty old school car with an elderly driver to the Hotel Bridge View where she found a nice clean room with white sheets and a fan over the bed. She had a shower, took her anti-malarial tablet, and climbed in between the sheets, ready for peace and sleep.

Meanwhile Lali showed Kiri her bed in the staff dormitory. It was hot and cramped, a small squeaky fan in one corner and a mosquito net over each bed, except the one they shared. Mother and daughter talked quietly in the dark for most of the night slipping effortlessly between English and Sinhalese. They drifted off to sleep for just a few hours as the sun rose above the horizon.

The next afternoon Penny walked over to the school. Term was starting in a few days time for the day girls but the resident girls and staff were there preparing already. Lali showed Penny round while Kiri had a long interview with Headmistress, who pointed out that this was a primarily English-speaking school.

She explained it was important for her girls to be fluent in English when they left school to join the world of their future. Headmistress was a strongly opinionated woman and that seemed to be her name – nobody called her anything other than Headmistress. Kiri had come prepared for both her roles – charity benefactor and also teaching assistant. She provided Headmistress with references from Mrs Woodward, who said what a hard worker she was, from Shelley who spoke of her language, business and IT skills, and from Mrs Bloom who described her as an honest person of great integrity. Kiri had to admit to Headmistress that she had very little experience with children, but was keen to rectify that and keen to learn and go on any courses that would be necessary. She'd already explained about her desire to be a nurse in years gone by and her experience as a health care assistant, and this had impressed Headmistress, as did her general attitude and demeanour. She planned to send Kiri on a first aid course at the local hospital and hoped she might be able to help in the sickroom at school as well as in the classroom alongside the trained teachers.

It was agreed that to begin with Kiri would work mornings only, for a small salary, with board and lodgings provided by the school, so allowing her the afternoons free to concentrate on her charity business. She would need to liaise with the council, designers, surveyors and contractors about the new dormitory and proposed nursery building, as well as finding a small house for herself and Lali to live in. Kiri was to start work on Monday in Class One, with Mrs Mendis, an experienced teacher as her mentor. She couldn't wait to tell Lali and Penny who were waiting for her outside on the veranda.

Penny only had a week to spend in Batticaloa and it flew by. She enjoyed working alongside the school staff getting ready for the new term, as well as talking with Kiri and the draughtsman who was drawing up building plans. She went with Kiri to meetings with the bank, the council and the solicitor who was going to communicate with Mrs Bloom. Penny couldn't believe the aptitude her apparently inexperienced friend had for business.

They went to see a small house for sale on some high ground just inland from the school. It stood empty and the overgrown garden looked in need of some love, even though the building was sound. The previous elderly owner had recently died and his distant family wanted it sold. It had two small bedrooms, a living room and an old-fashioned kitchen. A washroom and outside toilet were across an untidy yard. It was no palace, but Kiri thought it would do nicely and she and Mama would enjoy making it into their home. If there was any money left she hoped they'd build a proper indoor bathroom, and perhaps update the kitchen.

Soon it was time for Penny to board the train back to Colombo and start her journey home, carrying bundles of gifts for Clive and Hettie and Theo. The school gathered to wave her off and begged her to return soon. Kiri found it hard to say goodbye.

'I can't thank you enough for all you've done for me. How can I ever repay you?' she sniffled.

'You have repaid me already by bringing me back to this lovely island with its beautiful people. I will always want to return here, knowing how welcome I will be, and next time I want Clive to come too. I hope we can both come to the grand opening of Pearl House when your building is done,' replied Penny.

'That would be wonderful,' said Kiri, 'and perhaps Jean and Daniel will come too. I'll email you often with a progress report. Travel safely, my dear friend.'

43

Kiri soon felt at home, and quickly became part of the school. The younger girls loved her, especially when she read out loud to them in her lovely English voice. They read to her too and she soon realised how important books were to them all. How wonderful if she could help restock the school library which had been damaged in the tsunami! Kiri emailed Shelley who was on to it immediately, setting up a book recycling point at the hospital, and arranging for donated books to be shipped over to the school.

The design for the new buildings was agreed and builders were employed to do the work. The owner of the building firm, Sam, took on the job of project manager, and supervised his men as they laid the foundations. They worked long hard days in the heat, not bothering about a siesta, and only broke their day for lunch in the school canteen once the girls had finished and were back in class. Lali's cooking kept them going so they could finish the build in record time. Often in the afternoons Sam and Kiri exchanged ideas as they pored over the plans. They drank coconut juice in the site office or tea on the veranda and watched the project develop, sharing a common pride in the work being done, and enjoying each other's company. During those pleasant afternoons on the veranda, sheltered from the heat of the sun, they often let the conversation drift towards more personal matters.

Sam, short for Saman, told Kiri he was a widower with two grown-up sons, who worked with him on the building. Sam's wife had died in the tsunami – swept out to sea, and her body was never found. That was the hardest part for him, not knowing where she was now laid. His solution to grief was to keep busy. It was quickly apparent to Kiri that Sam had suffered much in his fifty years of life.

Sam had been brought up on the coast near Batticaloa where his father was a fisherman. His family were Sinhalese and in this Eastern Province they were in the minority. In the 1970s the Tamils tried to claim the region as part of the Tamil homeland. Sam was only 20 at the time and didn't get too involved with politics. He worked hard on a building apprenticeship and married Amanthi, his childhood sweetheart. They had three fine sons in quick succession. Kiri knew of his two sons on the building site at school and wondered about the third son who had never been spoken of before. She didn't ask, knowing he would tell her in his own time. He seemed to want her to understand his life story, as he was beginning to understand hers.

Amanthi and Sam led a simple but happy life with their three little lads, Dilvan, Dharma and Dilip. In their coastal village the Tamils and Sinhalese and Moors lived side by side in relative peace, respecting each other's ethnic and religious backgrounds, but in the larger towns they were aware of increasing tensions. They heard the concerns of their neighbours whose sons were being recruited to the Tamil Tigers and they feared for the future, protecting Dilvan, Dharma and Dilip as best they could. Kiri realised this was about the same time her own brothers had moved away, avoiding the troubles and leaving their mother in the safe hands of St Mary's School where she worked. Kiri had moved to Kandy by then so was less aware of the fighting in the east. St Mary's was a much smaller establishment in those days, but even then it had the same caring atmosphere. It had grown since, in both size and reputation, with two changes of headmistress along the way.

Sam and Amanthi were worried but proud when their eldest son, Dilvan, joined the Police Service. He was a good boy who wanted to serve his community, and at 18 he took the entrance exam and passed with flying colours – Sam said he looked so smart and handsome in his khaki uniform and black peaked cap and Kiri heard the pride in his voice. After training Dilvan worked locally to begin with but then he was promoted and moved to Trincomalee. This filled Amanthi with fear. The insurrection up north was escalating, with land disputes and personal vendettas rife, but Sam tried to reassure her that Dilvan knew his job and would be fine.

Kiri heard Sam's voice tremble when he told the rest of Dilvan's story. One day there was a suicide attack on the police station in Trincomalee where Dilvan worked. He was killed outright. A message came to them in Batticaloa the following day and Amanthi collapsed. Sam put her to bed and she didn't move or eat for almost three weeks. Sam took the two younger boys to work with him each day from then on and that's how they joined the family business. The boys missed their brother dreadfully and Dilip, the youngest, became very anxious. It worried Sam that the boy seemed to have lost his mother as well as his brother, and he told Kiri he feared he might never get over it. In time things improved, but Dilip always remained the quiet, sensitive member of the family. Sam was very proud though that he now helped as a volunteer support worker in his spare time, helping people injured in the tsunami.

'He's a good boy and getting stronger every day,' Sam said.

Dharma it seemed had fared somewhat better. He was nearly 18 when Dilvan died and had already started courting a pretty young girl from the village, with whom he spent every spare moment. After a respectful time of mourning they became engaged and married. Amanthi emerged from her grief to help organise the simple wedding but never really got her spark back after losing her first-born. She started to smile again only when their first grandchild, Tara, was born.

'Thank goodness she got to know Tara before she was taken,' said Sam, blinking back hot tears.

'I can tell by the way you speak of her how much you loved your wife. You are fortunate to have had that love, even if it was cut short,' said Kiri. She tried not to feel sorry for herself – for her loveless marriage and lack of children. Suddenly it wasn't about her any more.

'I have seen your sons at work and they are fine young men. You should be proud of them,' she continued, 'and as for little Tara, well you can't miss her. She's as bright as a little button and cheeky with it. She became one of my favourites in the class even before I knew she was your grandchild.'

Sam smiled bashfully when she said that, and Kiri worried she had got too personal too quickly with this shy, proud man, but somehow now he'd started to open up to her she didn't want him to stop.

'I can't think how you kept going after you lost your wife.'

'Kiri, I was not alone. So many people lost loved ones and we all struggled to survive, but we had to rebuild our community for the sake of our young people and the next generation. We have no choice but to carry on and help each other, whatever our background or politics. That's the one thing we can learn from a natural disaster – I just hope the politicians and the Tigers agree with me, but I fear the troubles are not over yet.'

44

Kiri's purchase of the little house on the hill went through quickly and soon she and Lali were setting up home there. Sam helped them put up shelves and make cupboards. Kiri bought simple furniture from the local store and Sam and his sons helped her transport it and shift it around the house. They added home touches and Sam's electrician put up ceiling fans for them. Kiri embroidered a sampler saying 'Home Sweet Home' and Lali set up the kitchen ready to produce home cooked meals for them.

Each evening on the veranda mother and daughter caught up with twenty-five years of ups and downs. They had missed so much of each other's lives and Lali realised with horror that Kiri had experienced more downs than ups in those lost years. Sam used to pass by from time to time with some excuse or other, and very cleverly often managed to do so at supper time. He invariably was asked to join them and Lali's chicken biryani with spiced coconut rice became his favourite meal, closely seconded by griddled seer fish. Mangoes grew on a tree in the front garden and they bought other fresh fruits from the nearby market for dessert. The garden was a small wilderness, but there would be plenty of time to tame that, thought Kiri, who wondered whether Sam might help with that too, and the very thought made her smile.

Her first term at school came to an end, and the new buildings were due to be finished during the Christmas break. The school was multi-faith but had a strong Catholic history so Christmas was celebrated as were other religious festivals through the year. Headmistress said this would give the girls a well-rounded view of the world and be useful to them in their adult life. Kiri emailed her charity trustees regularly and now told them about a grand opening planned for the New Year, to which they were each invited, so long as they could pay their own way.

Penny and Jean were both determined to get there and decided to try to combine it with a couple of week's holiday and a tour of Sri Lanka with their husbands. Penny tried to persuade Hettie and Theo to come, but Hettie had study commitments at uni and Theo found the dates clashed with his school ski trip to France, so he chose to do that instead. In the end Jean and Daniel could only get away for a week, which pleased Clive – he would much prefer two weeks alone with his wife than having to fit in with another couple.

The plan was made – the two couples would fly to Colombo then get the train across to Batticaloa for the opening, after which they would do their own thing for a few days. Jean and Daniel would relax on the coast before going to meet Penny and Clive for a trip down memory lane in Kandy. Meanwhile Penny and Clive would hire a car with a driver and go to Polonnaruwa and see the Buddhist temples there. They would move on to the rock caves of Dambulla, then go on to Sigiriya, where they would climb to the top of the magnificent rock fortress and see the frescoes of mysterious ladies on the walls. From there they'd get to Kandy to meet the others and stay at the Hotel Suisse, remembering old times when they swam in the pool after work. Penny longed to walk around the lake at Kandy and have a peep at the Lakeside Clinic again, as well as show Clive the Temple of the Tooth. She hoped they'd see the decorated elephants on their majestic parade past the temple, and maybe even get to the Elephant Orphanage. Jean and Daniel would then have to set off home, leaving Penny and Clive to go to the tea plantations at Nuwara Eliya. She hoped there would still be time to go to Anuradhapura and see the sacred Bo Tree and

Mihintale before returning to Colombo. Penny had wanted to do this for twenty-seven years. It would be the trip of a lifetime in relative luxury, compared with their trip on a student budget in 1978, and of course having Clive with her would be the icing on the cake. Penny emailed the schedule to Kiri for her approval.

Just before Christmas an extraordinary letter arrived for Kiri. It was from Charm, who had been getting updates about the charity and the building work from Mrs Bloom, her go-between. Charm announced that she had some time off work over the New Year period and she planned to do some travelling. She would very much like to visit the school and could be there for the grand opening if that suited everyone. If it was not too presumptuous she said she would like to offer her services to cut the tape at the opening, give a speech and sign some autographs. She went on – 'I know you may think this forward of me, but if you invite the press along I think I may be able to bring valuable publicity to your charity and even spread the word overseas. Also the girls at the school might find it exciting.' She assured Kiri she had no wish to steal her thunder and would not be offended if her idea was rejected – it was just a thought. She signed her letter 'With kind regards, Charm Diamond.'

What a bizarre offer, thought Kiri. Her first reaction was a definite 'no'. She thought about it, puzzled over it and fretted, as her feelings about the idea went back and forth. It weighed heavily on her as she tried to sleep at night. In an ideal world she never ever wanted to meet Charm, the woman who had cast such a shadow over her marriage, but she wondered if that was a selfish thought. The woman actually didn't seem too bad and in their recent contact she'd been very reasonable. She needed to talk this over with someone she trusted.

One afternoon, sitting with Sam on the veranda, it all came out. He knew about the problems of her marriage, and how difficult life with Raja had been, so he seemed the ideal person to share her doubts with. She showed him the letter.

'What do you think?' she asked him.

'It's a hard decision, Kiri. On face value it does seem a generous offer and some publicity might be a good thing. Would you be able to cope with her showy profile, and is it the right image for your charity though? Only you can decide, but I do think you should run it by Headmistress before you write back. She's a pretty wise old bird and will give an honest opinion.'

Kiri found Headmistress in her study. She didn't want to share too much detail about her personal life, so gave a potted version of the past, and then asked her advice on how to reply to the letter.

Headmistress replied thoughtfully, 'I'm not sure about a full-scale show-business affair for our opening, but some publicity would be good on many levels, and not simply financially. Mmm,' she pondered. 'It would be an exciting treat for the girls and I think if we retain control and handle it with care, we can accept her offer. We need to have some in-put about what she says in her speech and be able to check she hasn't got a hidden agenda alongside this kind offer. Why not tell her we are considering it and keep the lines of communication open?'

So, still dithering about her decision, Kiri entered into a more personal exchange with Charm by email and set the rules of engagement for this momentous meeting. Raja would have been astonished at the ease with which these two old love rivals communicated, she thought. She even felt the two of them developed a degree of mutual respect.

Planning for the event went well. Rooms were booked for Penny and Clive, and Jean and Daniel at the Hotel Bridge View.

Local dignitaries were invited and catering was arranged. Sam and his men put final touches to the buildings and the school grounds, and erected a flagpole upon which they hung a flag, made by Lali and appliquéd with the logo of Pearls across the Sea. The girls made bunting to decorate the fences and walls.

With two days to go Shelley emailed to say she was coming with Andy and they'd booked a room at another hotel nearby. They would be bringing messages from Mrs Bloom and Mrs Woodward and their other friends. Coming with Andy? thought Kiri. I wonder – no, surely not.

45

The day of the grand opening arrived and Lali helped Kiri dress in her best turquoise sari for the occasion, folding and tucking the pleats with great skill. Kiri's eyes were bright and her skin and hair shone as she anticipated seeing her friends again on this fine day. Her excitement was mixed with anxiety. She hoped this was normal anxiety.

The six English visitors had arrived in town the night before and were all getting on well. Daniel and Clive seemed to have developed a new level of friendship now they were older and appeared to be best buddies. Despite the evidence they saw of tsunami damage they were all in happy holiday mode and were thrilled at the preview they got of the new dormitories and nursery. They fussed over Lali and Kiri and congratulated them on all they had achieved.

They arrived for the opening ceremony before most of the local guests, and chatted comfortably with parents, and with children practising their English. A local photographer snapped away, recording the scene under Headmistress's strict direction. Local councillors and businessmen arrived soon after and giggling school girls showed them to the special seats reserved for them on a small stage erected by Sam. Headmistress was about to stand up to start proceedings when there was a sudden flurry of activity at the school gates, and a cohort of press cars swept into the dusty car park, followed by a huge, chauffeur-driven, silver Mercedes. A murmur spread through the crowd, followed by a gasp as Charm Diamond emerged from the shiny car, wearing a stunning scarlet-red dress, the highest high-heeled shoes Kiri had ever seen, and a pair of Jackie Onassis style dark glasses. She looked every bit a film star, with a vast retinue in tow and her own photographers.

Kiri was the only person who didn't seem surprised. She stepped forward and greeted the glamorous celebrity and introduced her to Headmistress, who managed to appear in complete control on the outside, whilst feeling quite agitated inside. It was more of a circus than she'd hoped for but she decided to go with it. Once everyone had settled down Headmistress began the official opening, by paying tribute to Kiri and her charity team. Kiri shyly thanked everyone for coming and for their support. She gave a special thanks to their wonderful builders and sneaked a smile to Sam before introducing their special guest, Charm Diamond, a supporter of their charity and all the way from India, who had kindly come to do the official cutting of the ribbon and to declare the new school buildings open.

Kiri went back to stand with Sam as Charm stood and smiled at the awestruck crowd. Cameras clicked and flags were waved. In a clear voice she made her simple but effective speech, which Kiri had already vetted of course.

'Headmistress, ladies, gentlemen and children, I am delighted to be with you on this special day at St Mary's School, to support the Pearls across the Sea charity and to congratulate all concerned on the hard work they have done. I know this school has a fine reputation, with an excellent staff and Headmistress, a reputation which has only grown since the awful damage and losses suffered last year. Now it has good-quality buildings in which to continue the excellent work it does with the girls of Batticaloa and the younger boys and girls in the nursery section. None of this would have happened without the love, care and commitment of one special woman, and that woman in Kiri de Souza. I congratulate Kiri and thank her on your behalf and now it gives me great pleasure to declare the new buildings officially open.'

She leaned forward and cut the red ribbon with some enormous scissors that Headmistress had found for the job. Charm turned her best side to the wall of cameras and seemed pleased with herself – this charming event would look perfect when she recorded it on her website. The role of charity benefactor would impress everyone back home, especially her new lover, she thought.

The little crowd cheered and clapped and more cameras flashed and clicked. As they did so, Penny watched Kiri slip her hand into Sam's, and he slid his arm round her waist and kissed the top of her head tenderly.

Penny nudged Jean and whispered, 'I think Kiri has found another project to work on now.'

46

Once the celebrations were over and the holidays ended, term got underway and normal life returned to the school. Pictures of the grand opening, including a shot of Kiri and Charm shaking hands, were posted on the school notice board for all to see, and a fulsome article appeared in the local paper describing Kiri as the guardian angel of St Mary's School.

Kiri enjoyed her care work with the smaller nursery children and the classroom work with the older girls, under Mrs Mendis's supervision. Lali was a good companion to live with in their little house and Sam was a regular visitor between work commitments. When the school building was finished though, he found he often had to go away to work and could be away for weeks at a time. Kiri missed him terribly when he was away. She had tasted true love for the first time and never wanted to let him go. Sam remained practical and every time he left they had the same conversation.

'Kiri, you know I must do this work even if it takes me away from you. It is my family business and I still need to provide for the family as well as help to rebuild our country. I will always come back to you – you know that don't you?' he reassured her.

'I know, but I still worry something will happen to you especially when you have to go up to the north. I couldn't bear to lose you now I have found you.'

Each time he went away she became filled with fatigue and anxiety. Her mood dipped down low and she fought to stay positive. She found life in Sri Lanka harder than she'd imagined. The temperature got hotter as the year progressed and her sleep was disturbed by hot sweats and bad dreams. The temperamental ceiling fan made things worse. Frequent power cuts upset her and she missed her favourite British TV programmes. She listened to the BBC World Service on the radio at night to keep in touch and looked out for letters from her friends. Penny and Shelley wrote regularly from the UK, which helped, and Mandy wrote from Canada as promised.

Kiri's other frustration was with the internet. She'd bought some second-hand computers for the school office but was having great difficulty with her internet connection which was slow and sporadic to say the least. Power cuts seemed to mess up the whole system and it took ages to recover documents. She often had to call in IT support from one of the parents, a well-meaning father who wasn't much better at it than she was and was himself rather slow. She was often without internet connection for days at a time and she worried she was missing important messages. Mandy's letters got further and further apart, and by summer had stopped completely. She never did email Kiri as they'd hoped, and Kiri wondered why.

Towards the end of the summer term Headmistress called Kiri into her office.

'Are you alright, Kiri? You look pale and tired,' she asked.

'I'm fine, thank you. It's just been a long term and I'm ready for a holiday,' replied Kiri.

'That's good, because I have something to say to you. I am delighted with the aptitude you have shown for teaching. The girls respect and admire you and you seem to really be able to get through to them, even the most traumatised and the most difficult girls. I would like to recommend that you go to teacher training college in the autumn and become a fully fledged teacher. What do you say?'

'Oh, I don't think that's for me,' replied Kiri. A little wave of anxiety passed through her. 'It would be too much. I couldn't study as well as do my other duties.'

'Don't worry. We'd rearrange things this end, and you would do your teaching practices here under our supervision. You're half way there with the work you already do here and I'm sure you can do the course. Just think it over. The college need an application by the end of the month.'

Sam came home a few days later and she told him about Headmistress's idea. He was thrilled at the suggestion.

'Wow Kiri, that's great. What a compliment for Headmistress to have such faith in your ability. She's right you know, you'd make a fine teacher. In ten years' time you could be headmistress yourself when she retires. How's that for a thought?' He chuckled at the very idea.

'It's too much for me, Sam. I know my limitations. I get so tired these days, especially when you're away so much. I can't do it,' said Kiri.

'I thought the word can't wasn't in your vocabulary. You have already proved you can do anything you set your mind to. I would be so proud of you. Give it more thought, Kiri. Don't throw this opportunity away. By the end of the year, when this big contract is done, I will be able to work more locally if that would help.'

Lali was similarly encouraging, as were the teachers she worked with, especially Mrs Mendis. Kiri wrote to Penny to ask her advice and tried to explain her reticence. It was hard to explain her feelings in a letter without sounding like her old pathetic self – the self she thought she'd left in England. Even Penny didn't seem to realise how hard she was finding life in Batticaloa. Penny just replied that with Sam by her side Kiri could achieve anything she wanted.

'I'll be out to visit you in January. That's going to be an annual event from now on. I take my duties as a trustee and as a friend very seriously you know,' she wrote.

Kiri took long walks along the sea front with Sam, trying to gain strength from holding his hand in hers and from the beautiful tropical sea which always soothed her. By the end of the month, and with Headmistress's help, she submitted her application. Anxiety hovered over her for the summer holidays, but Sam came home as often as he could and helped to damp it down. Headmistress rearranged a nursery timetable to fit in with lectures at the nearby college and Mrs Mendis went back to teaching her older class on her own. By September there was no turning back.

47

Kiri was the oldest student on her course, but her young colleagues were very kind and tried to include her in their activities. There were only three young men on the course and all the rest were women. She made friends with a couple of them, Gabi and Aruna – just girls themselves she thought, and not much older than the children they'll soon be teaching. They reminded her of herself at their age – pretty and lively and bright, and they made her feel old. Kiri did enjoy talking to them about how Sri Lanka had changed over the years since she'd been away and in return they were fascinated by her life story and loved listening to her talk about England. Gabi and Aruna both had ambitions to go to England one day, and Kiri let them dream of a fine future just as she had once done. She had to bite her tongue and hold back the words she longed to say – that the grass is not always greener on the other side.

As for her college work, Kiri coped well. Her life experience worked to her advantage and she was even able to help Gabi and Aruna and their young friends with some of their projects. Kiri did get very tired and Sam was still away a lot, but Headmistress stood by her word and helped her as much as she could, personally supervising Kiri's teaching practice. All went well until end of term exams loomed. Kiri hadn't taken an exam since she was at school and although she knew her work, and was conscientious with her revision, she feared the exams would overwhelm her. Lali made her soothing herbal tinctures and teas to relax her each evening after college and Headmistress gave her tips on exam technique, but the fear grew into panics. The jumping heart and tight chest disturbed her sleep and she woke early each morning with panting breath. She started to skip college lectures.

'I can't do it. I'm going to leave' she announced to Headmistress one morning.

'Are you sure? You can get through this. Lots of people get nervous at exams. You really know your stuff. Don't let a couple of three-hour exams stop you. It'll all be over by next week and the Christmas holidays will be here then. Sam will be home and you can have a good rest.' Headmistress didn't show her disappointment at her protégée's reaction. She'd thought she was made of sterner stuff.

'I knew it would be too much for me from the very start,' replied Kiri. 'I don't know why I allowed you all to persuade me.'

'Now, let's not give up so easily. We can speak to the doctor to get some mild medication to calm you and we can speak to your tutors and get some allowance for extenuating circumstances. They know you are a very different type of student and I suspect they will allow more weight to be given to your course work and less to the written exam if we ask. The teaching profession needs people like you with life experience, as well as the bright young things. Will you let me speak to the tutors and see what I can come up with?'

'If you think it's worth it, OK,' said Kiri.

'It's worth it,' replied Headmistress.

48

Somehow she did it. Kiri sat her exams with a little help from the drops prescribed by the local homeopathic doctor – she'd told Headmistress she didn't want to take any strong medication. The tutors agreed that her course work was excellent and they would allow that to be taken into account in her end of term marks.

The last day of term came and Kiri collapsed on the way to college to collect her results. She just went down in a deep faint – heavy as a corpse, crashing to the pavement. She bumped her head as she landed and passers-by couldn't rouse her.

They called for an ambulance and she was taken to hospital. Lali and Headmistress were phoned and took a taxi immediately to be by her side when she woke up. She was kept in with a diagnosis of exhaustion and concussion and still felt woozy when Sam arrived at her bedside the following day.

'I was so worried when I got Headmistress's message,' said Sam, 'How are you feeling?'

'A bit better and a bit foolish to be honest,' replied Kiri. 'I'm so sorry to have worried everyone and caused such a fuss. I just want to go home. I need to rethink things. I've been doing too much and I need to cut back. I obviously can't cope.'

'No quick decisions till you feel better,' said Sam. 'After a good rest the world will look better again. They say I can take you home in a day or two, just as long as you are looked after, and believe me, between Lali and me you will not have to do a thing for the rest of the holidays.'

'I don't know what I have done to deserve you. Thank you. Penny is coming to stay next week. Do you think it's too late to cancel her? I won't be much company for her like this.'

'It's rather short notice. Let her come – she'll have booked her tickets and she doesn't take much entertaining – she always cheers you up. It might be good for you to see her and to talk things through with her.'

'Perhaps you're right,' said Kiri. She hesitated. She lowered her eyes to hide the moisture gathering in them. She spoke again. 'There is something else, Sam. Now I want you to keep calm, but they've found a lump.'

'A lump, where?' Sam looked alarmed.

'In my other breast. It's small they say and very superficial, but they think I need tests. Mr Pereira the breast surgeon came to see me this morning and he's ordered a scan for this afternoon. He wants to take the lump away tomorrow morning, under local anaesthetic – they don't want to give me a GA after my head injury, but they say it'll be OK with a local and I've agreed,' said Kiri, trying to sound brave.

'Oh no. Perhaps it's nothing,' said Sam. 'I'm sure it'll be fine. Hadn't you noticed anything?'

'No, nothing.'

They sat in silence, holding hands until Kiri went for her scan. As she lay on the examination couch Kiri thought of Pauline and her dignified death. If this is my time I hope I can be as gracious as Pauline, with Sam by my side. She felt surprisingly calm now that Sam was back from the north and the realisation dawned that she had achieved most of her dreams in the last year – she had returned to Sri Lanka and found her mother again, she had made a difference to the children of St Mary's and made new friends there and most of all she had found love. If that is my life complete I must accept it, she thought and she closed her eyes as the scanner whirred around her.

49

Two days later, with a small tender wound in her breast Kiri was allowed home. Sam collected her and treated her like a porcelain doll until he got her back to the house and settled her in an easy chair. He left her in Lali's tender care and went back to his own home with a heavy heart, fearful that his new love might be taken from him.

Christmas Day arrived and everyone tried to look cheerful. Sam spent the first part of the day with his sons and granddaughter, then later drove to Lali and Kiri's house with a little bag of presents for them. Kiri had painted a tree sprig white and decorated it with coloured ribbons made from scraps of fabric. She topped it with a cardboard star – her very own Christmas tree. It had a small pile of presents under it and it made her think of strained Christmases in England with Raja. This Christmas was meant to be a happy one for once, but here again a shadow was hanging over it. Lali had bought a chicken which she roasted with spiced vegetables and while it cooked they opened their presents.

Sam gave Lali a new cooking pot and a bunch of wild flowers. Lali gave him a home-baked coconut cake, wrapped in brown paper tied with raffia. Kiri got a new blouse from Lali and Lali received a pair of leather sandals in return. Then Sam presented Kiri with a little box, wrapped in silk. As she opened it he spoke,

'Kiri, this is a special gift for you.'

She unwrapped it carefully and as she did so he asked her, 'Kiri de Souza, will you marry me? I love you very much. Will you do me the honour of becoming my wife?'

Kiri looked at the beautiful sapphire stone set in a gold ring and sighed.

'No Sam. I cannot marry you. The answer is no. I love you too but I can't be your wife.' She laid her hand on her breast. 'The answer is no, but I will always be your friend and your love. That will never change.'

Nothing Sam could say would change her mind and they picked at their roast chicken with little enthusiasm. All Lali's efforts for a wonderful meal were in vain and Sam took the leftovers home to Dharma, his wife and Tara. He insisted that Kiri kept the ring and she agreed to wear it on her right hand, as a token of his love.

* * *

Penny arrived after Christmas, not knowing the sadness she was coming to. She expected great joy and celebration, just like last year, and was upset to find a quiet house and a subdued Kiri greeting her. After tea she dared to ask the obvious question,

'What's going on Kiri. Things don't seem right here. Talk to me.'

Kiri did her best to explain the strain of her course, her collapse and finally the breast lump. Then she confessed,

'I've been so stupid. I took too much on. I shouldn't have listened to them all. They persuaded me to take the teaching course and I couldn't cope. I knew I couldn't, but I allowed myself to be seduced by their flattery. I got blasé and stopped my tablets. I didn't go to the clinic because I felt fine. The tablets made me hot and I couldn't sleep. I was so tired and I needed my sleep. I am such an idiot and now I've ruined everything.'

'Hang on now. Keep calm. Let's wait and see what the surgeon says at your appointment. When do you get your results?'

'In two days' time – will you come with me to the clinic?'

'Of course I will.'

'Whatever the results I am stopping my teaching course. It's not worth it. I was happy as a teaching assistant and my pride in not letting everyone down has been my downfall. I should have been happy with my lot. I was in a good place and I've ruined it all with foolish ambition, and the worst thing is that I've hurt Sam. He asked me to marry him, on Christmas day, and I said no.'

Kiri wept in Penny's arms. Penny held her tight – she knew she had her own news to tell Kiri, but now was not the time.

'But you love Sam, why did you say no,' she asked.

'He has already been widowed once. I can't put him through that again. We will always love each other, married or not, and I know he will still be there for me. I can't complicate his life more than necessary.'

'I think you've already complicated his life, Kiri, and he has willingly accepted the bad times with the good. I think he'll accept in sickness and in health too, don't you?'

'We'll see, but I'm not making a decision till I know what's happening.'

Two days later the women sat in Mr Pereira's office waiting. Kiri was waiting for her death sentence, while Penny was waiting for a miracle. Mr Pereira arrived clutching a folder of notes and quickly got to the point. Somehow he lacks the charm of Mr Rees, thought Penny, but he does seem efficient.

'We have your results and the news is mixed,' he announced. 'We have found the lump to be cancerous I'm afraid, but the good news is that it was very small and we have removed it all. The interesting thing is that the histology looks like a new primary and not a secondary spread from your last tumour.' As an aside to Penny he added, 'It was very well differentiated on histology and we've classified it T1 N0 M0.'

Penny sensed he was pleased and allowed herself to relax a little. Kiri didn't understand.

'How can another cancer be good news?' she asked.

'It means you will not need chemotherapy and the problem has been mostly dealt with by the excision biopsy – in effect it was a lumpectomy. On the downside I would like you to restart your tablets – you know, the ones you stopped a few months ago, and we will want to keep a much closer eye on you in clinic,' he said and allowed himself to smile.

'I don't believe you. That's all I have to do? I thought you were going to tell me I was dying, but you mean I can live – I can really live with this?'

'Yes, you can live. We would like you to have some radiotherapy to be on the safe side, but I think we can be positive about your future.'

Sam was waiting for them outside in the car. He hardly dare ask the results but knew he needed to know what had gone on in that office. Penny gave an explanation as clearly as she could and explained the plan. Kiri just sat staring into the distance while it all sank in, but was jolted back to the present by a big bear hug from Sam.

'We can deal with this, my darling. We'll face this together and you'll be fine with the treatment. It could have been so much worse. If you had not collapsed the tumour might have been found too late. Fate has handed you a lifeline.'

Kiri hugged him back and made herself try to believe his words.

'Come on, let's go home. We need to tell Mama the news – she'll be waiting for us.'

50

Penny and Kiri spent some good days together talking and sharing their thoughts. Kiri went to see Headmistress and explained the whole story, and together they wrote her letter of resignation to the college.

'I hope you understand. I should have been satisfied with my lot. I was happy and I pushed my luck too far,' said Kiri. 'There's just one thing – can I ask you for my hours back as a teaching assistant?'

'You most certainly can. We would love to have you back as soon as your treatment is over, and once you've had a rest. You can start again after the Easter break if that suits you. We're not letting you escape from our school – you are much needed here,' said the smiling Headmistress.

Penny was worrying about the letter she had brought from Mrs Bloom and had delayed handing to Kiri. Now that things were sorting themselves out she knew she had to give it to Kiri and hoped it would not shake her confidence once more. One evening after supper when they were alone and Kiri seemed relaxed, she chose her moment.

'Now things are more settled there's I have something for you. I've been waiting to tell you that I have a letter from Mrs Bloom with some news in it that might upset you.'

'Oh no, is she ill? What is it?' asked Kiri.

'No. Read it first then we can talk about it,' said Penny.

Dear Kiri

I have asked Penny to deliver this letter to you rather than post it, so I hope you are reading it with her alongside you for support. There has been a development here which relates to Raja and his estate.

It has come to light that before he died Raja fathered a child to another woman. Her name is Ria Silva and they had been having an affair for some years prior to his death. I believe they split up just before his accident and before she knew she was carrying his child. Penny may well be able to give you more details but the reason I have become involved is that she is making a claim on his will for child support. The legal position is complex and rather than allow her to take the case to court I have suggested I discuss the situation with all the known beneficiaries of Raja's will.

I have already been in correspondence with Rupesh and Charm, and now it is your turn to give your views. At risk of leading you against your will, Rupesh and I have come up with a plan.

Rupesh feels that this has nothing to do with Charm or you and should be dealt with by the Coomaraswamy family. He does not wish you or your charity to suffer in any way. If you agree he will arrange a monthly payment to go to the mother to support the child who has been named David. This will be funded by Rupesh from his third of Raja's estate, anticipating that in due course he will inherit further funds from his own very elderly parents. Rupesh's wife Mandy is in agreement and a reasonable sum has been suggested until the boy, David, is 18 years of age. We are hopeful that Ria Silva will accept this arrangement. Rupesh seems to be a quite remarkable man, I'm sure you'll agree.

Once you have had time to digest this and perhaps talk to Penny about it, please will you email me or write with your view? I do want everyone concerned to be happy with the decision and I will draw up appropriate legal documents and a contract with the woman. I am sorry to have spoiled your holiday with this news, but you did need to know.

Wish my good wishes

Hilary Bloom

Kiri turned to Penny with eyes wide open.

'Have you read this?' she asked.

'No but I know what it's about,' said Penny

'Read it. It's incredible. That man still cannot leave me in peace. He still troubles me from the grave. Whatever next?' Kiri put her head in her hands. 'A child – a boy. Poor little boy. Mrs Bloom says you know more details, so tell me all.'

Penny relayed the whole story, as told to her by Mrs Bloom:

Ria and Jack met regularly after her separation from Raja. Ria had apparently poured her heart out to Mrs Bloom and tried to explain. She told her she found the comfort of Jack's body had helped her through the dark days after Raja's death. Her affair with Raja had spanned over eight years and they'd only split up a short time before his accident. She tried not to but she missed him dreadfully, even though their last meeting had been so awful, when he'd lashed out at her viciously. She couldn't even grieve publicly and she was paying the price for her dark secret. Only Jack seemed to understand her loss.

She realised her contraceptive implant had time-expired some weeks earlier. She'd neglected replacing it, what with the upset of the assault and the split-up, but at her age she wasn't too worried – fertility in your forties was undoubtedly falling off, and she'd made an appointment for the next family planning clinic shortly after the funeral.

After the funeral Jack told her she seemed different – distracted and off colour. He hoped with patience and time the old Ria would return – feisty and strong-willed, or he might have to find a younger model. He'd teased her but she thought he really meant it. Ria kept going home early to bed and was off her food, tired and listless. Jack was unimpressed.

The clinic doctor insisted on doing a pregnancy test even though Ria swore it wasn't necessary. The test was positive. Ria had no idea of dates, having had no cycle since the implant was inserted. She was in her forties and had never been pregnant before. Raja had no children and even before the implant, when they'd played Russian Roulette with their contraceptive methods, she had never conceived. She found it hard to believe she'd been caught out.

Ria convinced herself the baby must be Jack's, even though she suspected he wouldn't be interested in fatherhood. She realised this was to be her one and only chance of motherhood and her Catholic upbringing made it hard to even consider a termination. She spoke to the clinic counsellor and decided she must keep this precious gift. She would find a way to manage even if Jack left her when he learned of her condition.

Ria kept it from Jack at first and they carried on much as before. Once she understood it she coped better with her morning sickness and hid it from her lover. She was tired, but actually felt even more sexy in pregnancy than before and Jack happily reaped the benefit of her surging hormones.

One night he commented how wonderful her breasts were – fuller and rounder than ever. Her skin seemed smoother and her belly softer. She'd had a dating scan by then and was feeling happy and proud of her body in this new role of creation, so taking a deep breath she made her announcement. The dates were borderline, but she convinced herself the baby was Jack's and hoped he would offer her financial support, if not emotional. She told him the baby was his.

Jack, to his credit, rose to the occasion, once he'd got over the shock. He promised to stand by her and understood her decision not to terminate – he was even a little bit proud at the thought of becoming a father, and arranged to move out of his hospital flat and into Ria's place so he could help her. The next few weeks and months passed in easy domesticity for the couple and Ria stayed well as her belly grew. Their friend, Helena, at first horrified, got used to the idea too and prepared herself for the role of god-mother.

Ria's relationship with Jack was good as she approached term. In October, a little earlier than expected, she went into labour with Jack at her side, mopping her brow and offering encouragement. Eight hours later she delivered a fine baby boy, weighing in at 7 pounds 3 ounces. The boy had dark hair and dark skin – when he arrived on this earth he was unmistakably Asian.

Kiri gasped and hung her head. Penny continued the story.

Jack was horrified and confused. He'd looked at David's spiky black hair and stroked his own light brown curls. He felt he'd been misled and that night he walked out of the maternity ward and went home to clear his stuff from Ria's flat, leaving her alone with her son.

In the end it was Helena who stood by her. She stayed with her and helped with the night feeds and looked after mother and baby in those early days. Ria was in a state of shock and could hardly raise herself from her bed when baby David cried for attention. It took weeks for her to regain her strength, but she did manage to breast feed David and gradually she formed a bond with her beautiful baby. She worried about how she would cope both physically and financially. She struggled for the first year and, unable to work, her money ran out quickly. The allowance from Enrico's parents stopped abruptly and with no discussion. Maternity benefit was insufficient for their needs and it was Helena who eventually suggested she had to do a formal paternity test before asking the Coomaraswamys for help.

This was where Rupesh came into it. Helena contacted Mrs Bloom and she arranged to get a sample from Rupesh. After comparing it with David's DNA they were able to confirm that the baby was indeed Raja's. There was hardly any need for that, Ria had said, you apparently only needed to look at David to know who the father was.

Jack never did come back – he moved south for a job in Guildford. He wrote to Helena from time to time to ask how Ria and David were, but said he just wasn't ready to bring up another man's child. He never contacted Ria again.

'David is now 15 months old and growing fast. His mother loves him very much and would be grateful for the financial support Rupesh is offering. What do you think?' asked Penny.

'Poor little boy. Stupid, silly woman,' said Kiri. 'It was her at the funeral wasn't it – the woman in black at the back. I thought I recognised her from the picture in Raja's study. Ria Silva, eh? All those cheques made out to her name. You'd have thought she's already had enough money from Raja and now she wants more. I certainly won't give her anything, even if we do have to go to court.'

Penny was worried Kiri was going to block the plan Mrs Bloom had so carefully arranged.

After a long, silent pause Kiri spoke again, 'A baby boy – it's not his fault. The poor child mustn't suffer. Are you sure Rupesh is happy with this? I need to speak to him, and to Mandy too. It's no wonder Mandy's letters stopped – she didn't know what to say to me. What a mess. Raja will continue to lurk in the shadows of my soul forever. I will never really be free of him. He will always be a small worm burrowing in my brain.'

Kiri couldn't sleep that night. The worm in her brain wouldn't stop wriggling and twisting. She ran through a telephone conversation she'd had with Rupesh that evening over and over again. Rupesh sounded totally genuine in his desire to help baby David. How could he deny his own nephew, he'd said? If circumstances were different he was sure Raja would have loved the child, and why should an innocent child suffer?

If circumstances were different he might have loved my child, thought Kiri. She'd thought of her own lost baby every day for a quarter of a century and though the ache was less raw, it never went away. She allowed herself a night of 'what ifs' then in the morning she rose to a new day.

Penny came over for morning tea on her last day in Sri Lanka and Kiri gave her a letter to deliver to Mrs Bloom, agreeing with Ru's plan and wishing the child well. The worm was still again.

'I think you've said the right thing. It will sit well with you over the years to come,' said Penny. 'Let's go for a long walk along the beach. I want to breathe the sea air and take the memory of it back to England with me tomorrow.'

They walked and talked and said all they wanted to say to each other, and Penny asked if she could come back again next New Year.

'Yes please,' said Kiri. 'I want you to come back here whenever you can. I want you to see me well and content with my lot for many years to come. I hope Sam will be by my side and we'll grow old together. I'm planning to tell him all about this latest development after you've left.'

51

Sam was disturbed at how emotional Kiri was about the news of baby David. Yes, of course it was a shock to her, but the way she allowed news of his existence to bother her so much only revealed to him how much damage Raja had done to her in the past. He saw how acutely she still felt the loss of her own child. He'd long since realised that beneath her capable exterior was a fragile soul, which she most often covered up successfully, but not always. He loved her all the more, knowing the effort she put into living a normal life, and was pleased he could help her with his own strength.

Sam dutifully drove Kiri for her radiotherapy treatments, and she gradually settled down again, fretted less and seemed more confident as each day passed. She told him how much she was looking forward to getting back to school and being with the girls in the classroom once more. She enjoyed playing and reading with Tara, who became her surrogate grandchild. The young people give me energy and hope, she told him one day, but he'd already seen that with his own eyes.

Sam stayed at his house and she stayed at hers, and though they saw each other every day, they never spoke of the sapphire ring on Kiri's right hand. Tara sometimes asked to look at it and liked to try it on, even though it was much too big for her dainty hands. Kiri told Tara to take great care because it was a very special gift to her from her very special grandfather.

'Do you love my grandpa?' the girl asked one day and Kiri replied that yes she did.

'Love him like I love him, or like mummy loves daddy?' Tara pressed on.

'Both,' replied Kiri, truthfully.

* * *

It was Christmas the following year before Kiri really felt well and fully in control again. Her clinic check-ups were all fine, she was tolerating her tablets better and was happy being a teaching assistant in Mrs Mendis's class again. Sam worked locally and sent one of his boys to supervise any long-distance work, rather than going away himself. On Christmas Day Sam came over for his Christmas meal, much as he had the year before, but when it came time to exchange presents Kiri jumped in first and presented Sam with a small box wrapped in silk.

'Sam,' she announced standing before him, 'will you do me the honour of becoming my husband? Will you move in here with me and Lali and stay with me for the rest of our lives – that is if you still want me for your wife?'

Sam opened his box and saw a solid gold band.

'Nothing would make me happier. Of course I still want you to be my wife. I knew you were worth waiting for,' he replied. He stood up and kissed his fiancée – such a long, loving kiss that Lali had to look away. Sam slipped Kiri's ring off the fourth finger of her right hand and slipped it on to her left hand.

'There,' he said. 'It looks much better there. But men don't wear engagement rings so I can't wear mine till we're actually married. We'd better get on with it quickly before I lose the ring.'

'Don't you dare lose it – anyway who says men can't wear engagement rings?'

Kiri took his strong, workman's hands and tried to squeeze the gold ring on to his left hand ring finger. It didn't fit. She pushed and shoved and licked the gold to lubricate it, but it just didn't fit. They started to chuckle then laughed out loud at the ludicrous scene. Sam wiped tears of laughter and joy from his eyes,

'We can get it enlarged or swap it for a bigger one, don't worry, and meanwhile I promise I really will keep it safe. We'll book the service and it'll be on that finger before you know it.'

Lightning Source UK Ltd.
Milton Keynes UK
UKOW031608120513

210551UK00004B/20/P